Panic flickered in he
second before she m......... ....
care of myself and my child, Mason. For
God's sake, I'm a doctor."

"This has nothing to do with you being a doctor or a competent woman," Mason said, his blood boiling. "It has to do with the fact that a crazed killer murdered one of your patients and may come after you."

His statement must have sunk in, because her face paled in the moonlight spilling through the car. He clenched his hands to keep from pulling her into his arms and comforting her.

She didn't look as if she would welcome his comfort.

"I did the math, Cara. We were together nine months ago. So unless you jumped into bed with another man right after I left—"

"How dare you imply that," Cara bit out.

"Then tell me who the father is."

Cara massaged her stomach again as if to protect the baby inside. "Mason—"

"Just tell me the truth," he said on a pained breath. "Is it mine?"

A long heartbeat passed, then she whispered, "Yes."

RITA
HERRON

NATIVE COWBOY

HARLEQUIN®
entertain, enrich, inspire™

To Sue and her cowboy boots!

Recycling programs
for this product may
not exist in your area.

ISBN-13: 978-0-373-74717-7

NATIVE COWBOY

www.Harlequin.com

Printed in U.S.A.

ABOUT THE AUTHOR

Award-winning author Rita Herron wrote her first book when she was twelve, but didn't think real people grew up to be writers. Now she writes so she doesn't have to get a *real* job. A former kindergarten teacher and workshop leader, she traded storytelling to kids for writing romance, and now she writes romantic comedies and romantic suspense. She lives in Georgia with her own romance hero and three kids. She loves to hear from readers, so please write her at P.O. Box 921225, Norcross, GA 30092-1225, or visit her website, www.ritaherron.com.

Books by Rita Herron

HARLEQUIN INTRIGUE

861—MYSTERIOUS CIRCUMSTANCES*
892—VOWS OF VENGEANCE*
918—RETURN TO FALCON RIDGE
939—LOOK-ALIKE*
957—FORCE OF THE FALCON
977—JUSTICE FOR A RANGER
1006—ANYTHING FOR HIS SON
1029—UP IN FLAMES*
1043—UNDER HIS SKIN*
1063—IN THE FLESH*
1081—BENEATH THE BADGE
1097—SILENT NIGHT SANCTUARY‡
1115—PLATINUM COWBOY
1132—COLLECTING EVIDENCE
1159—PEEK-A-BOO PROTECTOR
1174—HIS SECRET CHRISTMAS BABY‡
1192—RAWHIDE RANGER
1218—UNBREAKABLE BOND‡
1251—BRANDISHING A CROWN
1284—THE MISSING TWIN‡‡
1290—HER STOLEN SON‡‡
1323—CERTIFIED COWBOY**
1329—COWBOY IN THE EXTREME**
1336—COWBOY TO THE MAX**
1390—COWBOY COP**
1396—NATIVE COWBOY**

*Nighthawk Island
‡Guardian Angel Investigations
‡‡Guardian Angel Investigations: Lost and Found
**Bucking Bronc Lodge

CAST OF CHARACTERS

Detective Mason Blackpaw—Tracking down ruthless killers is his job, but will he be able to save the woman he loves and his unborn child when they become the target of a demented serial killer?

Dr. Cara Winchester—She has dedicated her life to saving women and children, but now she and her unborn baby are at risk and she must trust the man who broke her heart in order to protect them. Can she guard her heart against falling for the native cowboy again?

Reverend Webber Parch—Would he use God to justify killing those he deems sinners?

Alfredo Thompson—Would he kill the mother of his child because she gave their baby up for adoption?

Julie and David Davidson—Would they kill an innocent woman because they feared losing their adopted child?

Les Williams—Is this bitter war veteran killing women because of his PTSD?

Farr Nacona—Could this staunchly raised Native American be demented enough to punish women by death for what he perceives is their sin?

Prologue

She had to find out if her baby was okay.

Nellie Thompson pressed the accelerator, pushing her beat-up sedan to the limits as she veered onto the back road leading to the Bucking Bronc Lodge.

The people at the Winchester Clinic in town said Dr. Winchester lived on the ranch. But this section seemed deserted. Dark.

Isolated.

Panic clawed at her. Had she taken a wrong turn?

Fumbling with the directions she'd scribbled on a napkin, she tried to make out her own jagged writing, but it was too dark to see.

Her headlights caught the image of a wooden sign ahead. A sign that welcomed her to the BBL. Arrows told her the main lodge was to the left. It housed the counseling center and on-site clinic. Dr. Winchester's cabin was supposed to be to the right. She swung on to the dirt road, tires screeching and spitting gravel.

Dr. Winchester would know what to do.

She had helped her before. She would help her now.

But she had to tell her about the threats. The man's eerie voice…

She heaved a breath, pushing at the tangled hair on her cheek as she glanced in her rearview mirror. She thought she'd seen a car a mile back. Thought someone was following her.

Had she lost them? Or was she just being paranoid?

No…the truck had been too close. But where was it now?

Suddenly a loud popping sound rent the air. The car bounced, jolted forward, then rolled over a rut in the road.

Fear clogged her throat. Her tire had blown.

The car jerked and sputtered out of control. She pressed the brakes but the car spun sideways.

She pumped them again, but instead of slowing the car seemed to speed up. A cry caught in her throat, and she stomped the brakes one more time, then clenched the steering wheel in a death grip as it careened toward a boulder.

She swung the vehicle to the left to avoid it, but the car skidded off the road, trampling brush and bushes and bouncing over more ruts. She gripped the steering wheel tighter, struggling to regain control, but it was no use.

The front bumper slammed into a tree and the car screeched to a stop. Her head jerked forward and hit the steering wheel, and her world faded to black.

Seconds or maybe minutes later, she stirred, her vision blurred. Trembling from the impact, she reached for her purse.

She had to get her phone and call for help.

But someone wrenched her car door open. Relief warred with fear as a man pulled her from the seat. She blinked in confusion. Was he going to help her?

Something glittered in the dim light. A gold chain around his neck.

Then the shiny blade of a knife flashed in front of her face, and terror shot through her.

"Let me go," she shouted.

But his fingers tightened on her arm, and he dragged her toward the woods. She kicked and fought back. She had to get away from him.

A hard blow to his kneecap, and his grip on her loosened. She screamed for help then turned and ran. She had to make it to Dr. Winchester's cabin....

The terrain was dark, though, the night sounds ominous as she plunged through the bushes. The creek rippled nearby, but she stumbled over a tree root and fell.

The sound of crackling twigs and a man's cursing echoed in the air, and she pushed herself up and trudged on. She cut a path toward the creek, praying she was almost at the doctor's cabin, but her foot hit a tangled vine and she lunged into the brush. Her hands scraped rock and scrub brush, and she tasted dirt.

Then he was on her. His rancid breath bathed her

face as he grabbed her hair and flipped her over. She tried to scream, but one hand gripped her neck, choking her, while he raised the knife with the other.

She kicked and tried to throw him off, clawing at his hands to release her.

But the knife blade plunged into her stomach, and she choked on another cry as death whispered her name.

Chapter One

Three days later

Detective Mason Blackpaw watched the guard close the prison doors behind Pruitt Ables and breathed a sigh of relief that the *Slasher* case was finally over. Ables had been the missing link in their investigation, but once they'd realized Robert Dugan, the man who'd viciously killed a half dozen women, had a half brother, the pieces had fallen into place.

Mason exited the prison with a satisfied smile. He was a cowboy, a loner and a cop. He spent most of his days tracking down criminals.

His job was his life and that was the way he liked it.

No ties. No one to nag him about not being home when he was on a case. No one to expect him to be something he wasn't.

Except for the law enforcement agencies. Tracking had come so natural to him that he was called in on high profile missing persons and most wanted cases.

But now that he and Miles McGregor had locked up the sociopath and his accomplice, they'd decided to take some much needed R and R. Miles was headed to his new ranch with his son and new wife, and he had decided to devote some time to the troubled boys at the Bucking Bronc Lodge.

He checked his watch, then jumped in his SUV and drove toward the BBL. He'd promised Brody Bloodworth, the founder of the operation, that he'd teach the kids some survival skills as well as tracking techniques.

An hour later, he sat astride his favorite chestnut and introduced himself to the small group of twelve- to fourteen-year-olds. Ray was thirteen, had been beaten over and over by his old man and had a bad attitude. Wally was twelve and had lost an eye in a freak accident. Pablo had been in and out of foster homes and juvy.

And Carlos…he had been a hero of sorts when the *Slasher* had taken some of the kids and Jordan Wells, Miles's fiancée, hostage a few weeks ago.

"Ready to go?" he asked.

The boys nodded, although Ray looked surly and Wally a little unsure in the saddle. He'd keep an eye on him, maybe ask Johnny Long, the rodeo star of the group, to spend a little extra time working with the kid on riding skills and building his confidence. "We're riding out to the creek on the south end," he said.

He led the troops while Carlos held up the rear.

As they rode, Mason pointed out landmarks, the different varieties of plant life on the property and how to use the sun as a compass.

When they neared the creek, they climbed down from their horses, and he gave them a short lesson on herbs and plants that could be used for medicinal purposes. They hiked into the woods several hundred feet, and he pointed out some poisonous berries and explained how important it was to know the difference between what was safe to eat and what wasn't if you were ever stranded in the wilderness.

"That's what the Indians do, ain't it?" Wally asked. "They make medicine from plants."

"You're an Indian, aren't you?" Pablo asked.

Mason forced a smile. "Yes, I'm part Comanche. And yes, many herbal medicines and cures originated from Native American culture."

He was proud of his heritage, but he'd also encountered prejudice at times. Shocking that it still existed but it did. God knows he'd suffered the brunt of it a few times over the years. The last time had been seared into his memory. He had the scars to prove it.

But the boys didn't need to hear that.

Late afternoon shadows slashed the treetops as they walked along the stream, and he pointed out beaver teeth marks on a log and a coyote's paw prints near the water.

A squawking sound cracked the air, and he glanced up and noticed several vultures circling above a rocky section a little farther south. An uneasy feeling splintered through him.

Vultures circling… An animal was probably dead. Maybe a deer or another small animal.

He had to check it out.

"Guys, I'm going to ride over there and see what's going on."

Wally had been studying the beaver teeth marks. "We want to go, too."

Two of the vultures swooped down. "I'd better go alone," he said, hoping to shelter the boys from the grisly sight in case there was trouble.

Ray folded his arms with a belligerent look. "We ain't kids no more," he said. "I thought you were going to teach us survival skills."

"Yeah," Pablo said with a scowl. "How we supposed to learn to track if you don't show us?"

They were right. Besides, these kids were tough. He hadn't wanted to be treated like a child when he was a teenager.

"All right," he said. "But stay behind me. And do what I say."

The boys mounted quickly, then Miles led the posse along the creek. The sun was dipping lower, but the temperature had risen today, and sweat beaded on his brow as the acrid scent of death drifted toward him.

He peered through some brush where he noticed one of the vultures descend, and saw a mound of rocks beside a mesquite tree. Hmm…he'd expected a dead calf. Maybe a deer carcass. But he couldn't see from where he was.

He halted his horse, then motioned for the boys to wait.

"Carlos, stay here with them while I check it out." He dismounted, tipped his Stetson back and surveyed the area as he broke through the thicket of trees.

With each step he took, though, his gut tightened. The mound of rocks…the stones…the way they were placed…

He'd seen it before.

Dammit. It was a grave.

Sucking in a sharp breath, he scanned the area again, searching for anything suspect. For someone watching.

But an eerie quiet settled over the land, his shaky breath rattling in the silence, as he knelt to examine the stones. His cop instincts kicked in, and he removed a bandanna from his pocket and used it like a glove as he gently lifted two of the stones.

Anger shot through him.

A woman was in the ground, her eyes blank and staring up at him in death.

DR. CARA WINCHESTER RUBBED at her lower back as she closed the file on her desk. "Are you certain you want to go through with the adoption, Ramona?" she asked the Hispanic woman sitting across from her.

Ramona nodded, her expression torn. "I don't

know what else to do. How I raise this baby with no money for food?"

Cara offered her a gentle smile. She did what she could for her patients at the Winchester Clinic, but unfortunately she couldn't support them all financially herself.

"Why don't we set you up with an appointment with Sherese and she can discuss some options with you, maybe help you find a job."

"*Sí,* thank you, Dr. Winchester."

Cara walked her to the door, sympathy for the woman and the baby filling her. Her hand automatically went to her own rounded belly, and protective instincts surged to life.

Thankfully she had the resources to take care of herself and her child, but not every woman had the same good fortune.

Not that she didn't wish the father was in the picture…

Sadness washed over her as Mason Blackpaw's face flashed in her mind. She had fallen hard for the sexy cowboy cop, but in the end he'd trampled her heart and walked away without looking back.

Three weeks later, she'd discovered she was pregnant. She had considered calling him, but he'd made no bones about the fact that he didn't want to settle down. No, he'd spewed some nonsense about how a relationship with a white woman would never work. His argument had been so archaic she'd been furious.

Besides, she and the baby were a package deal.

And if he didn't want a white woman for a wife, he wouldn't want a baby with her, would he?

Her phone trilled, and she hurried to answer it, dismissing thoughts of Mason. But ever since she'd seen his picture in the paper with Miles McGregor, heroes because they'd solved a huge serial killer case, she hadn't been able to stop thinking about him.

Or remembering how heavenly it had felt to be in his arms.

Her phone trilled again, and she snagged it from her desk, tucking Ramona's file in the box to be refiled as she clicked to answer. "Dr. Winchester."

"Cara, it's Sheriff McRae."

Tension knotted her shoulders at his tone. "What's wrong?"

"I just received a call from Mason Blackpaw out at the BBL. He found a body on the ranch."

A shudder tore through Cara. Mason was at the BBL? And he'd found a body…

"Cara," the sheriff said. "Did you hear me?"

She swallowed back the sudden case of nerves assaulting her. She hadn't expected to ever see Mason again.

That he'd never find out about the baby. That she wouldn't have to deal with that kind of rejection.

"Cara?"

"Yes," she said, struggling to regain control. "Who did he find?" *Please, Lord, not one of the kids.*

"We don't have an ID yet. Blackpaw said it appears to be a young woman, probably early twenties. Can you meet me there?"

"Of course. I'll get my medical bag and be right out." Not that visiting crime scenes, if this was even that, was her favorite part of the job, but since she'd opened her clinic, she'd officially been named the assistant coroner for lack of anyone else to fill the job. Hopefully this was an accident, and she'd be able to avoid Mason.

The sheriff gave her the location, and she tensed when she realized it was close to her own cabin. Then she grabbed her purse and doctor's bag and headed to the front office. Sherese, her assistant nurse and receptionist, had already left for the day, so she locked up, then rushed to her Pathfinder.

The short drive to the ranch only heightened her anxiety. As if her baby sensed trouble, he kicked the entire way, reminding her that he was an active little boy and couldn't be forgotten.

That he would make his arrival in less than a month.

Would he look like his father? Have that strong Native American jaw? Mason's high cheekbones?

His stubborn independence?

Or…maybe he'd get that stubborn streak from her.

No, Mason had been stubborn, too. He hadn't cared enough to even call her after he'd left.

Because he hadn't loved her.

Dusk was setting, streaking the sky with orange

and red hues as she drove on to the ranch and veered down the road leading to the creek. The BBL covered hundreds of acres of ranch land with rich lush pastures for the cattle side of the operation and a quadrant designated for the horses complete with riding pens, stables, barns and cabins.

Ahead, she spotted Sheriff McRae's police car along with a minivan and a pickup truck.

She slowed, then parked and rubbed at her back again as she climbed from her SUV. The wooded area near the creek was at least a mile from the main lodge and camps that housed the campers.

What was Mason doing out here anyway?

Gripping her jacket around her in hopes that it might camouflage her condition, she grabbed her doctor's bag, heaved herself out of the Pathfinder, and walked toward the sheriff's car. She spotted McRae talking to Brody, then noticed Kim Woodstock, a counselor on the BBL, sitting on some rocks with a group of boys.

Had the boys seen the body, as well?

The wind picked up, swirling leaves around her as she neared the group. She gestured in greeting to Kim, then Brody and the sheriff.

"The body is over there," the sheriff said.

"Do you think it was an accident?" Cara asked.

He removed a roll of crime scene tape from the car. "Don't think so. She was buried and covered in stones."

Cara tensed. No, that didn't sound accidental…

"Come on," the sheriff said. "I know you want to look at the body while there's still plenty of light. Then we can move her to the morgue before dark."

Cara held her bag in front of her as he led her through the bushes. She braced herself to see Mason, but still her heart fluttered madly when she spotted his big body and that black Stetson. The first time she'd met him, she'd thought he looked like a renegade from the wild West.

He had certainly made love like one.

He was kneeling with his back to her, most likely examining the scene. But still he stirred her blood like no other man ever had.

"Detective Blackpaw," Sheriff McRae said. "Coroner's here to take a look."

Mason turned his head and spotted her, and shock lit his piercing dark eyes for a moment before he masked it. "You're the coroner?"

She nodded. She'd met Mason while she was doing a residency and volunteering on the reservation nearby. "I have a clinic in town now, but I also serve as assistant coroner."

His gaze raked over her, his jaw tightening, and she was grateful for the bushes between them.

But she knew her reprieve wouldn't last long.

Still, she had to play it cool. So she pulled on latex gloves, determined to keep this encounter on a professional level. For all he knew, she'd moved on.

And she had no doubt that he had. Mason was a sexual man.

The image of him with another woman taunted her. Made her want to scream.

But she'd be damned if she'd show that she was jealous.

"What happened?" she asked as the sheriff began to comb the area for evidence.

Mason turned back to the scene, and began snapping photographs. "Boys and I were out riding and I saw vultures," he said. "So I decided to check it out. When I saw the stones, I realized it was a grave."

Cara inched closer, the stench filling her nostrils. She'd smelled death before, but pregnancy accentuated her senses, and not in a good way. Then she spotted the woman's eyes staring up at her, cold and lifeless, and she had to swallow back bile.

"Is there some significance to the stones and the way they're arranged?"

"Yes. It's ritualistic, a Comanche tradition," he said in a clipped tone.

"So whoever buried her must have been Native American?"

"Probably, but we can't be sure. It could be someone obsessed with the traditions and rituals of the Indian people. Or even someone who killed the woman and wanted to make it appear like a Native buried her."

His tone was so curt that she realized he was going to play it cool, as if nothing had happened between them. Heck, he'd probably forgotten about her while she carried a reminder of him with her daily.

Fighting hurt and irritation, she took a deep breath. "You think she was murdered?"

He nodded, then moved aside. He had uncovered most of the woman's body. "What do you think?"

Cara gasped. The woman had definitely been murdered. Her stomach had been carved open in a brutal mess.

She was also one of Cara's patients.

Chapter Two

Mason tried to ignore Cara as she stooped down beside him, but her soft gasp disturbed him, and the sweet scent of her lavender soap melted into his senses, making it impossible.

He had to ignore his reaction, though. Hell, they had a job to do and nothing else mattered.

Not that he hadn't once lusted after her until he thought he'd lose his mind. Or that he'd been haunted by her tender voice whispering his name in the throes of passion.

Or that he'd wished he was different and that things could have worked between them.

But that was impossible.

She shivered beside him. She looked pale in the waning light, her eyes tormented as she stared at the dead woman in the ground.

Still, she was the most beautiful creature he'd ever seen, and she didn't bother to take time with her appearance. Her blond hair had been thrown up haphazardly on the top of her head and secured by some kind of clip, and she wore no makeup.

But her green eyes had always sparkled with intelligence, kindness and a sensitivity toward others that had drawn him to her from the start.

Except now they were filled with pain.

"Cara, are you all right?" he asked, suddenly concerned. It wasn't like her to get squeamish over blood.

"I know this woman," she whispered. "She was one of my patients."

Mason's pulse began to pound. "Then you might know who did this to her?"

Cara gently placed a hand on the woman's cheek as if to console her. "I'm so sorry, Nellie," she said softly. "So sorry. You didn't deserve this."

"No one deserves this," Mason muttered. "Who is she? Does she have family?"

Cara glanced at him, the shock subsiding slightly as if she realized she had to keep it together. "Her name is Nellie Thompson. And no, she doesn't have family." She opened her doctor's bag. "Did the boys see her?"

"Not like this," Mason said. "I told them to stay back while I walked ahead. I figured it was probably a dead deer or another animal." He paused, gulping back his own distaste. "They ran up and saw the stones and realized it was a grave. But I didn't uncover her until the counselor arrived. When she stepped aside with the boys, I photographed the stones and the way they were arranged, then the area surrounding the grave." He gestured toward the woods. "I'm going to conduct a wider search for evidence and hopefully pinpoint the spot where he murdered her."

She gestured toward the grave. "You don't think he killed her here?"

"No, but close by." He shined a flashlight across the terrain to the left, and she noticed a streak of blood dotting the ground.

"My guess is, he attacked her somewhere near the road, then dragged her to the woods to bury her." He frowned, thinking. "Now we need to figure out if she came on the ranch of her own volition, if they were together, maybe lovers, or if he brought her here against her will. Can you give me a firm time of death?"

Cara removed a kit from her bag and swabbed the woman's cheek where blood and dirt were caked.

"You said she was one of your patients?" Mason asked. "You live on the ranch?"

Cara nodded and continued to take samples from the woman's eyelids, hair and fingernails. "I offer medical services in the clinic on the BBL in exchange for a cabin."

"Maybe she was coming to see you," he suggested.

Her startled gaze flew to his, concern darkening her eyes. "I suppose that's possible."

"Was she ill?" Mason asked.

Cara shook her head.

"Then what was going on?"

"You know I can't discuss her medical information with you."

"She's dead, Cara," Mason said. "I think doctor-patient confidentiality can be waived to solve her murder."

Cara's mouth tightened. "I don't see how her medical information is relevant."

Anger knotted his chest. "Everything is relevant," he said. "This bastard was cruel." He gestured for her to look at the gruesome scene again. "We need to know the reason for the overkill."

Anguish strained her face. "So you think it was personal? Someone she knew?"

"Maybe...hell, I don't know yet." Mason studied the damage the killer had inflicted. "But it was violent. And the burial was ritualistic. Which means something triggered his rage, and that he might just be getting started."

MASON'S DECLARATION sent a shudder through Cara. He and Miles had just closed a terrible serial killer case, and now he thought there might be another serial murderer on the loose?

Had Nellie known the killer, or had she been chosen at random? If so, why kill her in such a brutal way?

The fact that the killer had butchered her abdominal cavity might be significant....

Leaves rustled behind her, and Cara startled and

stood. The baby chose that moment to kick, sending a spasm of pain down her leg, and she winced.

The sheriff strode through the woods, but suddenly Mason rose, his gaze latched on to her belly. She gritted her teeth, willing herself to remain calm, but his eyes darkened with emotions that made her chest clench.

She'd been in love with Mason ten months ago. She'd wanted a future with him, but he'd broken her heart, and she could not allow herself to fall for him again.

Or admit how much he'd hurt her.

"Cara?"

His gruff voice had once called her name in passion, but now a layer of confusion, shock and uncertainty underscored his tone. "You're pregnant?"

He didn't have to know it was his child, did he?

Then again, she had morals and she refused to lie.

"How observant," she said matter-of-factly. She gave him a look that dared him to ask more.

The sheriff broke through the bushes, his expression stony, and cut off Mason's response. "Blackpaw, you need to see this. I found her car, her purse inside."

Mason stared at Cara another full minute, but the sheriff was waiting, and she certainly didn't intend to discuss her pregnancy—or their situation—in front of him.

"Cara?" His gaze raked over her swollen stomach again, then he searched her face. For a brief moment, pain flickered in his eyes, then the moment passed, and his jaw tightened, making him look like a hardened, rugged cowboy cop.

"Go," she said. "You have a case to work, and I need to finish here and get Nellie moved to the morgue."

"You'll perform the autopsy?" he asked.

Cara pushed a strand of hair from her eyes. "Not me. I'll call in the county medical examiner."

"Make sure her body is processed for forensics," Mason said gruffly.

"Don't worry, I will." Her stomach churned. "I want whoever did this to pay."

"Also make a list of everything you know about her," he said. "Any detail might help us find the bastard who did this."

A debate began in her head. She knew he was right. But there were some parts of her life that Nellie had wanted to keep private.

"You coming, Blackpaw?" the sheriff asked.

Mason muttered a sound of frustration then left her alone with the body. Cara swallowed back the tears threatening to choke her as he disappeared into the woods. She couldn't take her eyes off his big sexy body. Couldn't help but remember the husky way he'd murmured her name in the throes of passion.

God help her. She was always saying goodbye to him.

What would he say when he learned the baby she was carrying was his?

Would he walk away from their child, too?

A DOZEN QUESTIONS pummeled Mason as he followed the sheriff to the car. Questions that had nothing to do with the case he should be focusing on.

Which was the very reason he'd walked away from Cara in the first place. He couldn't afford distractions. A personal life. To care about anyone.

But the image of her pregnant belly taunted him. Had she met someone after they'd ended their affair? He hadn't noticed a ring…but then he hadn't looked…

Was she married? Pregnant with her lover or husband's baby?

Mentally he ticked off the months they'd been apart. The dates they were together.

A little over nine months ago.

The air whooshed from his lungs in an agonizing rush. Could that baby be his?

"Her car went off the road up there," the sheriff said, gesturing toward the hill.

His voice jerked Mason back to the present. Dammit, if he didn't pay attention, he'd miss something important.

Leaves crunched beneath his boots as he trudged through the woods, and he dragged his head back to the case. He needed to be searching for clues.

He shined his flashlight along the ground, panning it across the bushes and terrain in case the killer had dropped something, maybe a button or glove, or some other evidence. Anything could be useful.

He spotted a patch of bushes that looked as if they'd been mangled, then knelt and discovered a partial footprint in the dirt that could have belonged to a man. A torn piece of clothing was trapped in a patch of thorns.

"Hang on a minute," he told the sheriff. "I think I found something."

The sheriff walked over and examined the print, then watched as Mason knelt and plucked the fabric scrap from the bush with some tweezers and placed it in a bag.

"I called in a crime unit from the county," the sheriff said. "I think we're going to need them on this one."

"You're right," Mason said. He was only one man. He couldn't do it all. "Make sure they take a plaster cast of this partial print. It might be helpful at some point."

A few more feet, and Mason spotted the small, rusted sedan crashed against the trees. The passenger side was intact, but the windshield was shattered, the driver's door stood ajar, and branches and limbs had caught on the roof and door.

"You already checked out the car?" Mason asked.

"Just a visual to see if anyone was inside, but I didn't touch anything." He gestured toward the handbag on the seat. "Left her purse there. Thought we'd want to photograph everything before we searched it and sent it to the lab."

"Good," Mason said, grateful the sheriff hadn't bungled evidence like some locals he'd encountered before. The smallest detail could prove to be important in analyzing the crime and catching this unknown subject, or UNSUB.

Mason shined his flashlight across the car interior. Blood dotted the dashboard and glass, and the seat had been torn as if someone had clawed at it.

Then he spotted a baby rattle that had rolled beneath the seat.

Hmm...did Nellie have a child?

"Look at this," the sheriff muttered.

Mason walked around the car and stooped down where the sheriff aimed his light on the tire. "Looks like it was slashed."

Mason's heart pounded. "Just enough to create a slow leak so the tire would blow."

The sheriff gestured toward the road with his hand. "Probably blew up there, she lost control, ran off the road and ended up here."

Mason noticed drag marks by the door and tried to visualize the crime in his mind. "The killer was following her. He watched her to crash. She hit her head, she's disoriented and he drags her out of the car." He paused, the images playing out. "At first she doesn't realize what's happened. She thinks this man might have stopped to help her. Then he drags her into the bushes and stabs her."

"But why?" the sheriff asked. "Does he know her? Did he choose her for some reason?"

"That's what I intend to find out." Mason snapped some pictures of the car and surrounding area, took several shots of the slashed tire, then retrieved the woman's purse and rifled through it.

"ID confirms she's Nellie Thompson. She was twenty-four, lives nearby. I'll send a patrol man over to search her house." He rummaged deeper and located her cell phone, but the battery was dead. He'd check it out, though. She might have had contact with her killer. Or if she was being followed by a stranger, she might have tried to call for help.

"Check the 911 calls and see if she phoned one in."

The sheriff nodded, then the sound of an engine cut into the quiet, and they made their way back to the body to meet the crime unit.

Cara was kneeling by Nellie's body again, her expression torn. He understood how much more difficult it was to have to work a case when it involved someone you knew. Someone you cared about.

Another reason he'd vowed never to get close to anyone again.

But she stood and pivoted, then walked toward the crime scene tech who was descending the hill, and his chest clenched at the sight of her pregnant belly.

He'd never imagined loving anyone again, not since the girl he'd fallen for when he was eighteen.

And he'd certainly never imagined having a child.

But a surge of longing hit him like a bolt of lightning during a storm.

Fool.

The baby might not even be his.

But what if it was?

Why hadn't she told him? And what would he do if it was his child?

CARA TOOK A DEEP BREATH as Mason approached. He looked larger than life as he strode up the hill, the evening shadows framing his silhouette like a tough cowboy from a movie set.

Except this scene was very real. And a patient and friend of hers was dead.

The crime techs introduced themselves, and the sheriff directed them to the burial spot.

"We found her car." Mason's jaw tightened as his gaze fell on her belly. "Her tire was slashed, then it blew, causing her to run off the road."

A shiver rippled up Cara's spine as she realized the implications. "So someone targeted her before the attack. He was following her."

"That's the conclusion I would draw," Mason stated, his dark eyes fierce. "The question is who."

Cara clenched her medical bag with a white-knuckled grip.

"Tell me everything you know about her, Cara. She was your patient, did she mention that anyone was bothering her? Maybe she had a stalker?"

Cara shook her head. Although she had felt like

someone had been watching *her* lately. Not that she'd seen anyone; it was just an eerie feeling every now and then that someone was behind her. Or that someone had been in the clinic.

She'd attributed it to the fact that her friend Sadie Whitefeather had had a couple of break-ins at the reservation clinic. Since the Winchester clinic wasn't in the best part of town, it might be targeted if someone was looking for drugs, too.

"Cara?"

She jerked her attention back to Mason. "No, she didn't mention anyone."

"Did she have a boyfriend? Lover?"

Cara chewed her lower lip. This was sticky territory.

But in light of Nellie's mutilated body, she had to help Mason find the woman's killer, no matter the cost.

"A boyfriend." She twisted her hands together. "But I don't think he would do this."

Mason quirked his mouth to the side. "I'll need to talk to him. Did she mention any other adversaries? Someone she might have upset lately? A coworker? Friend?"

She shook her head no, although Nellie's secret haunted her. What if it had something to do with her death?

"Did she work?"

"She was a waitress at a coffee shop, but she was taking classes to become a hairstylist."

"So no one in the class was bothering her? She didn't have a stalker from the coffee shop?"

She shifted, weighing the truth. "No. Not that I know of."

"Cara, please," Mason said, obviously picking up on her nerves. "Tell me what you know."

She hated to broach the subject, especially in light of her own condition, but she had to do everything possible for Nellie. And that meant finding justice for the brutal way she'd died.

"We need to talk in private," she said quietly.

His gaze shot to her stomach again, and she shook her head, warning him that her pregnancy wasn't important right now. While he and the sheriff had examined the car, Kim had driven the kids back to the camp, so she gestured for him to follow her to the rocks where they'd been sitting. When she reached the boulder, she sat down, relieved to take the pressure off her lower back.

Mason didn't sit, though. He stood and folded his arms, waiting.

God, he could be insufferable like that. Quiet, brooding and…dark. Intense.

Almost scary.

And sexy as hell.

"Cara?"

"Nellie recently had a baby," she said in a low voice.

He hissed between his teeth. "Dammit, I saw a

rattle in the car. You think this man kidnapped the child?"

"No, and the baby may not have anything to do with her murder, but…she gave the child up for adoption when it was born."

Mason's frown deepened, carving grooves in his chiseled tanned jaw. "And the boyfriend? Did he know about the adoption?"

Cara sighed. This hadn't been her secret to tell. And it could open a can of worms between her and Mason.

Still Nellie's mangled body taunted her. "He knew," she said in a low whisper. "But I…"

"You what?" Mason asked harshly.

"I think he changed his mind after the baby was taken away."

Miles released a curse. "Meaning he had motive."

FROM HIS PERCH on the hill, he watched the scene unfolding. That Indian cop uncovering the stones.

The bastard knew what they meant.

Did he know what the woman had done to deserve to die?

Why he had to take it upon himself to rid the world of unclean women like her?

Laughter bubbled in his throat as he spotted the sheriff with those crime guys. Let them look for evidence all they wanted.

Hell, he'd been careful. They wouldn't find anything he didn't want them to find.

He dug the toe of his boot into the dirt, wished it was that bitch Winchester's face. It was her fault he had to do what he did.

Her fault that Nellie had to die.

That the others would die just like her.

And then it would be Dr. Winchester's turn.

Yes, he would save her for last.

And he'd make her suffer.

Chapter Three

"I need the boyfriend's name, and the name of the adoptive parents," Mason said. "If Nellie's boyfriend killed her, he may have gone after the baby."

Panic flared inside Cara. She hated to violate any patient's privacy, but he was right. She couldn't allow a vicious killer to touch that innocent child. "I don't know his name, but it's in my files at the clinic."

Mason made a low sound in his throat. "All right, let's go."

Cara stood, fumbling with her bag, doubts needling her. "The timing seems off. It looks like Nellie has been dead for at least a day or two. Maybe longer. If someone had tried to kidnap the baby, the parents would have reported it."

"Maybe, maybe not," Mason said. "The killer may have needed time to find out the adoptive parents' names and address. Besides, we have to check it out. It's our only lead right now."

Cara blinked as more headlights appeared. The

ambulance had arrived to transport the body to the morgue. "Let me talk to the medics for a minute, then I'll go."

Mason followed her to meet the paramedics. "Wait until the crime unit is finished processing the body before you move her to the morgue," Cara said. "I took some samples as well to send to the lab."

The medics nodded in understanding, then followed her to the burial spot to confer with the crime unit.

Cara handed off the evidence she'd collected, and they signed the necessary forms for chain of custody. "Both the sheriff and I need to be notified of the autopsy results."

A female investigator named Erin made a note of it.

Mason took a few moments to detail specifics for the team to analyze, handed off a fabric sample he'd collected in the woods, and reminded them to process the victim's car and the stones.

"Maybe we'll get lucky and the guy left some DNA."

"I doubt it," a tall lanky CSI tech said. "Guy probably wore gloves…"

Mason frowned. "A loose hair, fiber from his clothing, even a partial print could be helpful. Hell, maybe the guy sneezed on the car or on her, or maybe she scratched him and we can lift DNA from her fingernails." He paused and handed the tech Nellie's phone. "Search her phone log and send me the names and numbers of her most recent calls."

The tech assured him they would be thorough, and Mason followed her up the hill to her car. Cara's back was hurting again, but she refused to draw attention to her condition so she refrained from rubbing it.

Still, when they reached her vehicle, she had to draw a deep breath before unlocking the door.

Mason gripped her arm. "Are you all right?"

"Yes," she said. "It's just Nellie...poor Nellie. And her baby...I'm worried about her." Nellie had loved her child and thought she'd done the right thing by giving her to a nice couple, a family. Was her little girl safe?

"I'll follow you to the clinic," Mason said. "Maybe you're right and this murder had nothing to do with the adoption or the child. But we have to explore every angle."

Cara shut out images of the brutal way Nellie had been left as she slid into the driver's seat. Knowing Mason was behind her gave her a small sense of relief. Although it also rattled her nerves in a different way and triggered memories she didn't want to dwell on.

Memories of the two of them dancing together in the dark. Of hot, loving nights and sweet mornings where they drank coffee and read the paper together.

Of the long lonely months since he'd left and the baby kicking inside her.

God.

They still had to talk about her pregnancy.

But first she had to find out if Nellie's child was in trouble.

SHE DEFINITELY wasn't wearing a ring.

Mason stewed over the implications as he followed Cara into town. Was she married, or did she simply not wear a wedding band? And whose baby was she carrying?

The instinct to confront her made him clench the steering wheel tighter. Surely if the baby was his, she would have told him. She was one of the most honest people he'd ever met.

Another reason he hadn't wanted to dirty her with his ugly world.

A sliver of disappointment wormed its way through him, but he swallowed it. He had walked away from Cara. He had no claims on her. No right to be jealous that she'd moved on with someone else.

The fact that she'd opened a clinic in town and helped with the kids on the BBL didn't surprise him, though.

She had loved practicing on the reservation, and probably still volunteered her time on the res with Carter Flagstone's wife, Sadie Whitefeather.

But as he wove through the small town, and he realized the clinic was in a low rent section, worry gnawed at him. He admired the bleeding heart aspect of Cara's personality, but he didn't like the idea of her working in a high-crime area.

Night had fallen, the dark sky making the area look sketchy and dangerous as she cut through an alley then a side street and parked in front of a weathered cement building with peeling paint, an awning that was tilted sideways and weeds choking the small patch of land.

A wooden sign with the name Winchester Clinic dangled in the breeze, Cara's name etched below it. She'd overcome obstacles that she hadn't wanted to talk about to earn her degree, and he hadn't pushed for answers about her past, although he sensed she had secrets she didn't want to tell.

But the fact that she'd struggled and overcome whatever demons she had in her past had only intensified his attraction to her.

Hell, he'd feared he was falling in love with her, so he'd had to keep his distance. Leave her while he could.

Besides, he'd been assigned an undercover mission, one that had taken him away for months. One he'd known would be dangerous and could have gotten anyone who'd been close to him killed.

Cara slid from her vehicle, clutching the door for support as she righted her pregnant frame. He stifled a curse as his body tightened.

Dammit, he'd never thought a pregnant body was beautiful, but Cara made it look almost…sexy.

Perspiration beaded on the back of his neck. Hell, what was wrong with him?

She was not his and never would be. He had to remember that.

But the past still taunted him with the possibility that her child might be his. As soon as he got the information they'd come for, he'd find out the truth.

He checked his gun in his holster, pushed himself from the seat, and followed her up the small walkway to the front door of the clinic.

Cara clutched the rail as she climbed the steps to the front stoop, then unlocked the door. Mason followed her, his cop instincts kicking in as she flipped on the lights.

In contrast to the weathered exterior of the building, fresh paint and colorful curtains made the interior look cheery.

But the office had been tossed. Papers were scattered all over the floor, and file drawers hung open, the contents rifled through.

Cara gasped, and Mason pushed her behind him, reached inside his jacket for his gun and lowered his voice. "Wait here—let me make sure the intruder's gone."

A banging sound echoed from the back. The wind whistled.

But he didn't hear voices or footsteps.

Still, that didn't mean the place was clear. The intruder might be hiding.

"How many rooms in the back?" he asked in a low voice.

"Two exam rooms, one on each side of the lab," Cara whispered. "My office is in the back."

He gave a clipped nod, once again gesturing for her to wait while he searched the premises.

The scent of antiseptic suffused him as he inched past the waiting room. Two more steps and he spotted the lab. Scale for weighing was in the corner. Gauze, bandages and other medical supplies were organized in jars on the counter.

The door to the medicine cabinet stood open, and vials had been overturned.

Whoever had broken in had been looking for drugs. No surprise in this neighborhood.

But why toss files in the front office?

Pulse drumming, he pushed open the door to the exam room. A sliver of the streetlight outside illuminated the room just enough for him to do a visual sweep.

At first glance, he didn't see anything amiss. Basic exam table, medicine cabinet above a sink, first aid supplies.

A thorough search and a moment later, he deemed it clear.

Keeping his shoulders squared, gun braced, he moved to the room on the left. He paused to listen before he opened the door, and gripped his weapon tighter as the banging sound echoed again. This room was dark, too, same basic layout except a few stuffed toys filled a basket in the corner and bright cartoon characters were painted on the walls.

But no one was inside.

Relieved, he sucked in a sharp breath, then stepped back inside the lab and crossed to the office. It was small and cramped with a filing cabinet and tiny desk, a bookcase with medical books on one shelf, toys and a jar of lollipops on another.

Empty, as well.

The slapping sound continued, and he tensed and whirled around, then stepped from the office.

Dammit. The intruder was gone, but now he knew how he'd gotten in.

The back door was open, flapping in the wind.

CARA HELD HER BREATH while Mason searched the building. She had worried about a break-in before, but in light of the murder, the timing aroused suspicion.

Careful not to touch anything, she visually noted the disarray on Sherese's desk. Thank God the break-in had occurred after hours and her assistant hadn't been here.

The day's patient files that hadn't yet been put away lay scattered in a mess. And the files in the cabinet had been shuffled through, pages tossed on the floor. It would take time to sort through them and see if anything was missing.

What had the intruder been looking for? A specific file? But whose?

And why?

The sound of Mason's footsteps echoed across the cement floor, then he appeared, tucking his gun back inside his jacket. "It's clear. But someone broke into the drug cabinet." He cut his gaze across the disheveled office and files.

"If they wanted drugs, why toss the files?" Cara asked.

"Good question." Mason folded his arms. "The back door was open. Looks like the lock was picked."

"I'll get it fixed," Cara said.

"You'll do more than that. You need some dead-bolts, a security system and cameras."

Cara shrugged. "I can't afford all that, Mason."

"Well, I can," Mason said. "I'll set it up."

Cara's heart pounded. "I can't let you do that."

Mason glared at her. "Yes, you can. Consider it a charitable donation."

Cara chewed her bottom lip, fighting the urge to argue, but decided to forgo her pride and conceded. She didn't know if Mason had money or not, but the clinic could use donations. She had major plans to expand the women's pavilion to offer medical and counseling services, a rape crisis hot line, and consultants for family planning. Eventually she wanted a children's wing, as well. But she needed funding to pull it off.

"Can you tell if anything's missing?" Mason asked.

Cara pushed her hair from her eyes and began to sort through the folders. "Not yet. I'll ask my assistant Sherese to check in the morning."

Mason nodded. "I'll call a locksmith and the sheriff and report this. He can send another team to process the rooms."

"That's going to be difficult," Cara said. "Do you have any idea how many people I see daily?"

Mason shifted, looking frustrated. "No. Getting his print may be a long shot, but we have to cover all the bases."

An image of Nellie's blood-soaked body taunted her. "Do you think this could be related to Nellie's murder?"

Mason shrugged. "It's possible. Maybe the killer was looking for the adoptive parents' names and broke into the drug cabinet to throw us off."

Fear slithered up Cara's spine, and she hurriedly glanced at the files on the floor, searching for Nellie's. But there were hundreds of pages, all in disarray, so she decided it would be quicker to check the computer.

"Let me find the information on Nellie's boyfriend and his address."

"Get the adoptive parents, too," Mason reminded her.

She suddenly paused. "Sherese turned the computer off before she left."

"Which means whoever broke in tried to get something off of your hard drive." Mason studied the screen. "It looks like he tried to access patient files."

Cara sighed wearily. 'They're password encrypted."

Mason shrugged. "That may be the reason he dumped the hard files." He placed his hand over hers. "Use gloves now so you don't contaminate the keyboard in case he left prints."

Cara's throat tightened.

Mason removed his phone from his belt and headed to the front stoop. "I'll call the sheriff and have him fingerprint the clinic, so we can track down the boyfriend."

Cara nodded. She just prayed that they found out who'd killed Nellie and that her baby was safe.

But what if the killer had been here at her clinic? She'd received hate mail before, mail telling her that they didn't need her kind of help. That she was encouraging women to give up their children.

But that wasn't the case.

Still, what if Nellie's murder and the break-in were connected?

Mason's comment about the ritualistic aspect of the crime troubled her even more.

What if the killer planned to strike again?

HE SIFTED THROUGH the files, smiling at how easily he'd copied them and hacked Dr. Winchester's password.

It really had been easy. People were so predictable. All he had to do was dig a little into the pretty doctor's past. And now he was in.

Sweet mercy. The list was longer than he'd expected.

The thrill of realizing he would replay the fun he'd had with Nellie made his body hot all over. Sweat trickled down his neck. Adrenaline churned. His pulse and heartbeat soared.

He lifted his bottled water and took a deep drink.

Nothing artificial would contaminate his body. He had flushed out the poisonous toxins long ago just as he had to flush out the poisonous women now.

Dr. Winchester had alphabetized the names, so he scrolled down the list. He could start in the order she'd presented them.

A laugh bubbled in his throat. No…that would be too easy. Too boring.

He would shake up the list. Keep the cops on their toes.

Let them wonder who would be next.

Chapter Four

Cara felt violated as the crime unit combed through the clinic. She had to protect her patients, many of whom came to her because they knew they could trust her.

Some were in terrible home situations, were dealing with abusive boyfriends or husbands, and others needed medical help as well as counseling. Single mothers, women who needed financial assistance, and unwed teenagers who had to make a difficult choice regarding their child's future—whether to keep the child or find an adoptive family.

Mason oversaw the crime unit, his gaze continually straying to her and her rounded belly. A confrontation was inevitable, but thankfully he was professional enough to leave their personal business simmering on the back burner for the moment.

After all, a young woman's brutal slaying was their top priority.

"We'll need your prints, ma'am," one of the crime

techs said. "Just for elimination purposes. We'll also need your other employees' prints."

Cara allowed the female tech to take her print. "I'll have my assistant Sherese come to the police station."

"What do you know about her?" Mason asked.

Cara frowned. "You mean, can I trust her?"

Mason nodded. "Do you think she might have stolen the drugs and made it look like a robbery?"

Cara released a sardonic chuckle. "No, Sherese is one of the sweetest, most honest, trustworthy women I know. She's not only had nurses aide training but she's a single mother raising a small child on her own."

"Maybe she needed the money and planned to sell the drugs?" Mason suggested.

"No," Cara said emphatically. "Her father was an abusive alcoholic. There's no way she would sell or do drugs. She actually helps counsel addicts when they come in."

"Sounds like you think a lot of her."

Cara nodded and wiped her fingers off on a towel. "I do. Now let's move on."

Mason studied her for a long moment, then started to speak but the crime techs interrupted. The male tech cleared his throat. "We're finished here, Detective Blackpaw. We'll get these to the lab ASAP."

"Thanks. I'll need to compare them to any prints we found at the murder scene of Nellie Thompson."

As the techs gathered their equipment and left,

a wariness settled over Cara. She wasn't ready to have the discussion about the baby.

"Cara?" Mason said in that gravelly voice that sounded like seduction.

She fought off a reaction and turned to the file cabinet.

"If the drugs were stolen to cover up the real reason the intruder broke in, and it's related to Nellie's death, the killer may be after Nellie's baby. I need to go."

Cara glanced at the printout. "His name is Alfredo Rodrigo." Cara grabbed her purse. "I'm going with you."

Mason glanced down at her belly. "No, this is police business."

Cara tucked the address into her bag. "Listen Mason, Nellie was my patient. I'm going to protect her choices and her child just like I promised."

She started toward the door, but Mason caught her arm. "You don't trust me to protect this child?"

His question lingered between them for a pained heartbeat. Cara had to wonder if he was referring to Nellie's little girl or the baby she carried.

"That's not the point," she said evenly. "This adoption was a private matter, Mason. I know Alfredo took it hard, but the adoptive parents were assured confidentiality. Having a cop at their door is going to upset them, and I can help smooth the waters."

Turmoil darkened his eyes, but a second later he

gave a clipped nod of acceptance. "All right, but let me take the lead with Rodrigo. Remember, he's a suspect in a murder investigation."

Cara sucked in a deep breath. How could she forget? She would never be able to erase the image of Nellie's butchered body from her mind.

THE URGE TO PUMMEL Cara with questions nagged at Mason as he drove from the clinic toward Rodrigo's address. But she looked uncomfortable and worried about Nellie, and she had just identified the body of a woman she knew, a woman who'd been brutally slain and whose death was obviously personal to her.

His questions would have to wait. At least until they'd talked to Rodrigo, and he decided whether the man was the suspect they were looking for in this homicide.

"Do you think we should call Alfredo to make sure he's home?" Cara asked.

"No, I want the element of surprise on my side."

"I'm telling you, he wouldn't kill Nellie, especially in such a vicious manner."

"Maybe not," Mason conceded. "But crimes of passion can turn ugly. And if he didn't kill her, he might know something that could lead us to who did."

Cara nodded, then turned to look out the window, worry knitting her face. For a moment, he was tempted to squeeze her hand to console her, but he had no right. Besides, touching her was too personal.

He had to guard against his emotions.

The town lights disappeared behind them, the landscape giving way to wilderness, scrub brush and the beauty of the Texas land. Small ranches and farms were interspersed between patches of deserted land rich with cacti, boulders and mesquites. He passed the sign for the local reservation where Cara had first volunteered.

Memories of watching her work with patients hit him, reminding him of the compassionate woman who had stolen his heart. He glanced at her, his gut tightening as moonlight spilled across her ivory skin and highlighted the rich tones of her hair.

Hair that he had lost himself in just as he had lost himself in bed with her.

Dammit. The very reason he'd had to walk away.

No one had ever turned him inside out like she had.

He'd vowed that no woman ever would again.

But now here she was working at the BBL, running a clinic in town, right in his face.

Hell, when he finished this investigation, he'd request a transfer. Texas was a big damn state.

But what if that child is yours?

Cara shifted, her hand automatically flying to her stomach when he hit a bump, and he silently chastised himself, then checked his speed. For God's sake, he needed to take it easy.

There was a kid on board.

One that might be his.

Sweat broke out on his brow as he turned down the road leading to Rodrigo's. His own father had been nonexistent in his life. Had deserted him and his mother the moment he'd discovered she was pregnant.

Hell, she had been both parents to him, though, had raised him on the same res where he'd met Cara. A couple of the men on the res had taken him under his wing and taught him to fish and hunt. Chief Pann had taught him to track.

They had served as his male role models, as opposed to the man who'd actually fathered him.

If this baby was his, what kind of father would he be? Cara hadn't told him about the child, so she must not want him in the baby's life.

That thought made his stomach knot.

"It's at the end of that street," Cara said as she pointed toward a graveled road.

Mason veered on to it and slowed as the car churned over the rocks and spit dirt. Several weathered cement houses lined the street, the yards unkempt, children's toys scattered on the overgrown, weed-infested yards.

He parked in the driveway and cut the engine, noting the beat-up pickup in the drive. A light burned in the front window, illuminating the front porch.

Cara opened her car door, and he jumped out and ran around to help her. But she was standing by the time he reached her, her gaze daring him to comment on her bulk.

"Remember, let me take the lead," Mason said.

"I'm telling you that Alfredo loved Nellie." A frown crinkled her eyes. "He's going to be devastated that she's dead."

Mason refrained from comment. If she was right, the next few minutes would be unpleasant, but breaking bad news came with the job. He'd learned to compartmentalize and not let it affect him, but Cara was too kindhearted not to be disturbed. After all, she dedicated herself to saving lives.

So did he, but in a different capacity. Although he had taken a life or two in the past. But only when necessary.

He was tempted to take her arm as they walked up the graveled path to the door, but she trudged forward, independent and determined to prove that pregnancy hadn't slowed her down.

They climbed the cement steps, and he knocked on the door. A moment later, an Hispanic man with shaggy hair wearing a flannel shirt and jeans opened the door. He rubbed at his unshaven jaw with a scowl.

"Alfredo Rodrigo," Mason said. "I'm Detective Blackpaw."

Cara pushed her way in front of him. "Can we come in?"

He frowned at Mason, his eyebrows arching at the sight of Cara. "What's going on?"

Cara gave him a compassionate smile. "Please, Alfredo, we need to talk."

His gaze shot between the two of them, then he gestured for them to enter. Mason immediately scanned the man's body for a weapon, but he appeared clean.

They stepped into a small living room with a faded plaid couch, a rickety coffee table laden with take-out wrappers and a pile of laundry in a wooden chair.

"What this about?" Alfredo asked in broken English.

"Nellie." Cara glanced at the kitchen. "Let's sit down."

She led the way and they seated themselves about a Formica table with plastic chairs.

"What about my Nellie?" Alfredo asked. "What's wrong?"

"When did you last see her?" Mason asked, ignoring Alfredo's question.

Alfredo rubbed his chin again as if thinking back, and Mason noticed a scar on his cheek that looked old, maybe from a knife. "Last week. Before I left town."

"You've been out of town?" Mason asked.

"I drive a truck, big rig, haul petroleum products." He tapped his foot up and down. "Tell me, is Nellie okay?"

Mason noted the concern in Cara's eyes, but forged on. "When did you get back?"

Alfredo stood, suddenly looking panicky. "This

morning, dawn." He crossed his arms. "Now, tell me about Nellie. Is she okay?"

Cara drew a deep breath. "No, Alfredo, I'm afraid she's not."

Alfredo's eyes twitched. "What wrong? Is she in hospital?" He started toward the door. "Tell me, take me to see her."

Cara stood and gently gripped his arm. "I'm afraid that's impossible, Alfredo. I'm so sorry."

"Nellie is dead," Mason cut in, determined to get a visceral reaction from the man. Cara's sympathy would only stoke his story if he planned to lie. "She was murdered."

Alfredo staggered backward, his expression pained. "No…not my Nellie…not dead."

"I'm afraid she is," Cara said softly. "I'm so sorry, Alfredo."

Tears welled in the man's big dark eyes. "No… you're wrong."

"She was murdered and someone buried her on the BBL ranch," Mason said matter-of-factly. "I found her body this morning when I was out riding."

Alfredo slumped into the chair and dropped his head forward, tears rolling down his face. "No…I talk to her. Try to get her to come back to me."

"You two broke up about the baby, didn't you?" Mason pressed. "You didn't want a child."

Anger flashed in Alfredo's eyes. "No it not like that."

Cara covered his hand with hers. "It's okay," she

said. "You can trust us, Alfredo. Just tell Detective Blackpaw the truth so we can find out who killed Nellie."

His startled gaze swung to Mason. "You think I hurt her?"

Mason made a low sound in his throat. "I think she got pregnant, you didn't want a child, then she had the baby and gave it away. Then what? You changed your mind?"

Alfredo's mouth thinned into an angry line. "It true at first I not want baby." He paced, his movements agitated. "I worry about taking care of child. Had no job back then." He rushed to the counter and grabbed his wallet. "But last month I get good job with trucking company." He yanked out ticket stubs and receipts, spilling them on the table. "See. I tell Nellie I take care of her and baby now, but she say it too late."

"And that made you mad, didn't it?" Mason said. "So you tried to force her to come back to you. What happened then?" He got in the man's face. "Did you say no, it was over? Did she tell you that you'd never get your kid back?"

Alfredo's face crumpled. "She did say it too late, that couple adopt our little girl." He choked on the last word. "But I promise her I still love her and want her back." He thumped his finger on the receipts. "See, these from my run. I leave last week, go cross country. Stop at a different motel each night. Gas up. Stay in El Paso last night. It all there."

Cara sifted through them, then looked up at Mason. "He's telling the truth, Mason. The receipts prove he wasn't anywhere near town or the BBL."

Mason sighed. Alfredo could have hired some-one to kill Nellie, but judging from the genuine-looking tears on his face and the fact that he didn't have much money, he didn't appear to be the kind of person to pay for murder, or be able to afford it.

Not in the heinous way Nellie had been killed. And if so, why would he bury her using a Coman-che ritualistic style?

"Where is she now?" Alfredo asked. "I want to see my Nellie."

Mason exchanged a look with Cara. "She's at the medical examiner's office," he said. "Does she have any other family we need to notify?"

"No," Cara said. "Her parents were killed in an accident a couple of years ago. They were all she had."

"Except for me," Alfredo said in a voice that cracked. "And I let her down."

Cara gently rubbed his shoulder. "We'll let you know when she's released so you can plan her fu-neral."

"What about the lawyer who handled the adop-tion?" Mason asked. "Did you have contact with him or the adoptive parents?"

Alfredo shook his head. "No, I don't even know who they are. Nellie didn't want me involved." His eyes darkened. "Why? You think they know something?"

Mason refused to admit that he was worried about the child. Of course, Alfredo had reason to go after the baby because he was the father.

But if he hadn't killed Nellie to get the baby, who had?

Unless Nellie had changed her mind about the adoption. What if she'd decided to reconcile with Alfredo? If she'd tried to break the adoption agreement, the adoptive parents would have been upset.

Upset enough to kill her to keep the child they considered theirs?

Chapter Five

Cara's heart ached for Alfredo. He and Nellie's situation mirrored so many others she worked with. They had been in love but mired in poverty, the strain of an unexpected pregnancy had come between them. By the time Alfredo had realized he wanted a family, it was too late.

But Nellie had made her choice with the best intentions of her little girl in mind.

"I'm so sorry, Alfredo," she said, then enveloped him in a hug.

He cried on her shoulder for a moment, then being a proud man, he pulled away, swiping at his tears.

"Please, Miss Cara, you will let me know when I can see my Nellie?"

"I will."

Then he turned to Mason. "You'll let me know who killed her?"

Mason nodded, then gestured to Cara that it was time to leave. She followed him out to the car, her heart aching for Alfredo. He had finally gotten the means to take care of the woman he loved but now he'd lost her to death.

Her baby chose that moment to kick, reminding her that her son's father was only a few feet away, and that she'd never given him the choice of whether he wanted to be a part of their child's life.

She'd been selfish in thinking only of her own hurt feelings. But at the time, she'd been certain he would have walked away.

Now she didn't know.

"He appears genuinely upset," Mason said as they settled in the car.

Cara winced as the baby pressed on her bladder. "I told you he wouldn't kill her. He doesn't have it in him to do what that killer did to Nellie."

"What about the adoptive couple?" Mason asked. "You heard Alfredo say he wanted her and the baby. What if Nellie went to the couple and asked them to forfeit the adoption?"

Cara frowned. "She knew it was final when she signed the papers."

Mason headed down the graveled road. "Maybe she did, but that doesn't mean her emotions didn't drive her to plead for her baby back."

Cara's throat tightened. "I suppose it's possible." In fact, sometimes mothers regretted their decision and later tried to back out of adoptions. But there was a window of time that allowed for that, and it had passed.

"The last time I saw Nellie she seemed okay with

her decision," she said. "In fact, I had convinced her to attend school and she'd signed up for cosmetology classes. She seemed excited about it."

"We have to talk to the adoptive parents," Mason said. "See if she contacted them."

Cara twisted her hands in her lap. She hated to upset the couple who'd adopted the little girl, but her clinic had been broken into. And if killing Nellie had been about the baby, she needed to make sure the child was safe.

"All right, they live in San Antonio. Do you want me to call them?"

"No," Mason said. "Like I said earlier, I want the element of surprise on our side."

Cara jerked her head toward him. "You think one of them killed Nellie?"

Mason shrugged. "I'm just trying to eliminate the obvious suspects at this point. The baby's real father and adoptive parents are closest to the case."

Cara smoothed down a wrinkle in her shirt, then handed Mason the address for the Davidson family and watched him program it into his GPS. She had dreaded telling Alfredo and confronting him. She wasn't looking forward to questioning the adoptive parents, either.

But Mason was right. Even if they hadn't killed Nellie, they were the logical places to start.

His phone buzzed, and he punched connect so she lapsed into silence.

"Tell him I'm on my way." Mason disconnected then swung the car back on to the main road.

"What is it?" Cara asked.

"The sheriff said his officer found something at Nellie's apartment that he wants us to look at."

Worry nagged at Cara as Mason raced toward the apartment complex. The building was old, the concrete units weathered, mesquites adding a touch of Texas character to the dismal surroundings. Mason noted the numbers on the building, found Nellie's, and he and Cara walked up to the apartment together.

The door stood ajar, two officers inside. "Emery Dothan," a young brawny officer said by way of introduction.

"What did you find?" Mason asked.

The officer gestured to the kitchen, and they followed him to a pine table where a sheet of paper lay. "It looks as if someone was threatening Nellie Thompson."

Cara gasped as she read the note.

Do you know where your baby is?

Mason frowned at the message. "So this was about the baby?" Mason murmured.

Cara gripped the table edge. "God, Nellie must have been out of her mind with worry."

"Did you find anything else?" Mason asked the officer.

The young man shook his head. "We checked her computer but so far nothing."

"No chat rooms? Social media contacts? Suspicious emails?" Mason asked.

"No. Her history is limited, mostly sites about educational opportunities."

"She was shy, not very computer savvy. But she had planned to go to cosmetology school," Cara said. "Only she never had the chance."

"Follow up with the lab regarding her phone," Mason said. "If he sent this message, he may have called her, as well."

"Copy that."

Cara paled as she and Mason walked back to the car.

"What was the lawyer's name who handled the adoption?" Mason asked.

Cara tucked an errant strand of her hair behind one ear and settled into her seat. "Regan Wurst."

Mason sank into the driver's seat and fastened his seat belt. "Call him and see if he's had any inquiries about the Thompson baby."

"Regan is a she," she said, then slipped her phone from her purse and scrolled through her contact list. A second later, she punched in a number.

"Regan, it's Dr. Winchester."

Mason focused on the road as he drove toward San Antonio, but he kept one ear on Cara's conversation.

"I'm calling regarding the Thompson adoption," Cara said. A pause. "Nellie Thompson was murdered. I'm working with the detective to find her

killer." Another pause. "We have questioned the father, and he has an alibi." Cara hesitated, and he
heard the lawyer talking, but he couldn't understand
her exact words.

"We're on our way to talk to the Davidson family now," Cara said. "But my office was broken into
and files rifled through, the Thompson file among
them. I need to know if you've had any inquiries
about the baby."

"No," he heard the woman say.

"No one has been to your office asking questions
about the adoption?"

"No."

"Okay, thanks, Regan. If anyone contacts you,
please let me know." Cara fiddled with her hair,
twisting a strand around her finger.

Was she nervous about the investigation, or had
she considered giving her child up for adoption?

No...Cara would never do that...would she?

"So she hasn't had any trouble?" Mason asked as
she said goodbye.

"No." Cara laid her head back against the seat and
closed her eyes. She must be exhausted.

He should have insisted she go home and rest.
Take care of herself and the baby.

But she was stubborn and wouldn't have listened,
not when she felt protective of the people involved
in this case.

Her breathing slowed, and a few minutes later he
realized she'd fallen asleep, so he drove in silence,

passing farmland and deserted areas until he reached San Antonio. The bright lights of the city gleamed against the darkness, traffic thick as evening picked up with the dinner crowd and nightlife.

He plowed through the streets, weaving through the downtown area and turning into the newer, more exclusive complex where the Davidsons resided. Judging from the gated community entrance and the sparkling lights adorning the neighborhood, the Davidsons had money.

How much had they paid for Nellie's baby?

And to what lengths would they go in order to keep her?

CARA STIRRED FROM SLEEP as Mason parked in front of the sprawling two-story Georgian home where the Davidsons lived. She had never been to their house, but Regan had relayed that the family was wealthy and would be able to give every advantage possible to the Thompson baby.

A small comfort to Nellie when she'd handed the little girl over. But she had loved her baby enough to want her to have a happy life and a bright future.

A wave of sadness washed over Cara at the loss of the young woman.

"Are you sure you're up for this?" Mason asked.

Cara nodded, reached for the door handle and pulled herself out. Mason hurried around to help her, but once again she made certain she stood on her own. She had been for months now. She couldn't grow dependent on him now.

Lights glittered along the drive leading to the portico, houselights glowing in the windows indicating the Davidsons were home.

They were probably finishing dinner and putting the baby to bed for the night.

Mason rang the doorbell, and she tapped her foot while they waited. A moment later a housekeeper in a maid's uniform opened the door. She introduced herself as Gloria. "Yes?"

Mason flashed his credentials and introduced both of them. "We need to speak to the Davidsons please."

Gloria's dark eyes flashed with concern. "Can I tell them what this is about?"

"I'd rather do that, ma'am," Mason said matter-of-factly.

She gestured for them to follow her through an expensively decorated foyer lavish with art and vases, but they ended up in a living room that actually looked cozy and kid friendly. Although the leather furniture was obviously pricey, a baby swing, infant toys and a bouncy seat gave it a homey feel.

She took a seat in the rocking chair in the corner while Mason stood, his gaze scanning the photos of the baby girl on the mantel. The sound of Gloria's voice and then the couple's drifted toward her, then Julie and Don Davidson appeared in the doorway, Julie cradling the three-month-old in her arms.

"Detective?" Don extended his hand and shook Mason's, but both he and his wife looked wary. "What's going on?"

"Please sit down and I'll explain," Mason said.

Julie clutched the infant to her chest as if she expected them to rip the baby from her arms. "Is this about Lacy?" Julie asked, her tone tinged with panic.

Mason cleared his throat. "Yes, ma'am, I'm afraid it is."

"No, you can't take her," Julie cried. "She's ours, it's all legal, we signed papers, we have rights."

Don held up a calming hand to his wife. "Is that the reason you're here?"

"No," Cara said, eager to console them. She understood the constant worry adoptive parents had that they might lose their child. "That's not the reason for our visit."

Julie and her husband exchanged a confused look. "Then why are you here?"

"Please sit down," Mason said.

The Davidsons huddled together on the sofa. Lacy started whimpering as if she sensed something was wrong, and Julie rocked her in her arms, soothing her with softly whispered words of love.

Nellie would have taken comfort in the way the couple loved her baby, Cara thought.

"Why are you concerned that we came to take the baby?" Mason said. "Had the mother or father asked for the child back?"

Don shook his head and Julie followed. "We

haven't heard from the mother at all. In fact, we've never even met. All communication was done through our attorney."

"Regan Wurst?" Mason asked.

The couple nodded in tandem.

"How about the baby's father? Has he tried to contact you?"

"No," they both said at once.

Julie's eyes widened. "Do they want Lacy back?"

"No," Mason said. "Why do you think that?"

"I've just seen stories about that happening," Julie said.

"It's all right, Julie, I promise you, that's not why we're here." Cara stroked little Lacy's soft dark hair. "Can I hold her?"

Julie looked wary, but nodded and allowed Cara to gently lift the baby from her arms. Cara rocked Lacy back and forth, her heart constricting when the baby looked up into her eyes and cooed.

"Please, Dr. Winchester," Julie said. "Tell us what's going on."

Cara glanced at Mason, and he cleared his throat.

"Where were you the night before last?"

Don narrowed his eyes. "At a work function until midnight, then in the hotel the rest of the evening."

"What kind of work do you do?"

"I'm a developer," Don explained. "I helped develop this housing community, and we've just opened up a similar one in Dallas."

Mason angled his head toward Julie. "What about you, Mrs. Davidson?"

Cara tensed. He couldn't possibly suspect sweet Julie Davidson of such a heinous crime.

Julie squared her shoulders. "Lacy and I were here. My mother came for a visit, and we took Lacy to the park that afternoon, then had dinner out and came home."

"So you both have people who can confirm your whereabouts?"

Don's mouth compressed into an angry line. "Yes. Now what the hell is going on? Why do we need an alibi?"

Mason heaved a sigh. "Because Nellie Thompson was murdered that night."

"Oh, my God," Julie gasped.

Don's eyes widened in shock. "You think we had something to do with her murder?"

"We're simply trying to work through the process of elimination at this point. If Nellie or the baby's father had pushed you to relinquish custody—"

"That would be motive," Don said as he reached for his cell phone. "Don't say anything else, Julie. I'm calling our attorney."

"Don," Cara said. "We're not accusing you of anything. We're just trying to figure out what happened to Nellie."

Julie took the little girl from Cara. "Regan promised us confidentiality, and we did everything by the book. Lacy is ours."

Cara squeezed her shoulder. "I know that, Julie. We're just trying to find Nellie's killer. And frankly, I had to make sure Lacy was safe."

Don clenched the phone, hesitating. "You think whoever killed Nellie might come after the baby?"

Mason cleared his throat. "At this point, we don't have any idea. But just to be on the safe side, you should be careful."

"We could take her away somewhere," Julie said, her voice stricken. "Maybe my mother's in Houston."

Mason shook his head. "Until the investigation is over, don't leave town."

Fury flashed in Don's eyes. "Then I'll hire around-the-clock security. No one is going to get our little girl."

Cara shot Mason an angry look. She didn't believe Julie or Don had anything to do with Nellie's murder any more than she thought Alfredo had.

And she hated that they'd frightened the couple.

After all, the murder might not have anything to do with the baby. It could have been a random killing.

MASON HANDED HIS CARD to the couple, then asked both of them to write down contact information to confirm their alibis. The couple was huddled together as they left.

"They didn't have anything to do with this," Cara said as soon as they stepped outside.

"You don't know that. Even with their alibis, they have money. Davidson could have hired someone to do his dirty work for him."

"But you heard what they said, and Regan confirmed it. Neither Nellie nor Alfredo contacted them about custody." Cara opened her car door. "Besides, the Davidsons have plenty of money. If there had been a problem, they could have hired a top-notch attorney to defend their position and won. There would be no reason to resort to murder."

Mason climbed in the car, and Cara slid into her seat and fastened her seat belt. "So if they had nothing to do with it, we're back to nothing."

"Except that we have a violent offender." Mason raked a hand across his jaw. Cara's rationalizations made sense. Both Nellie and Alfredo had been impoverished. And money talked. The Davidsons probably would have won the case if it had gone to court. "We need to take a closer look at Nellie, find out everything she did in the days leading up to her death."

His cell phone rang, and he connected the call as he pulled down the drive. "Detective Blackpaw."

"This is Dr. Tarrington, the ME working on the Thompson body. Dr. Winchester requested I contact you with my report."

Mason's heartbeat picked up. Maybe he had something helpful. "Yes, what did you find?"

"No forensics, I'm afraid."

"Cause of death?"

"Exsanguination. But that's where it gets interesting."

Perspiration beaded Mason's neck. "What do you mean?"

"This bastard didn't simply stab Nellie Thompson," Dr. Tarrington said. "He cut out her uterus."

HE WATCHED THE WOMAN cozy up to the man in the bar, her long black hair sliding over her shoulders like a dark curtain. She was flirting outrageously, sipping her third martini, lavishing attention on the poor guy who had no idea that she was nothing more than a common whore.

Not the mother she should have been to her child.

No, she'd thrown her kid away like it was an inconvenience, barely taking a day off from her busy work life and partying to find a couple who would take it off her hands.

And that bitch Dr. Winchester had helped her.

He sipped his bourbon and watched her lift a blood-red fingernail to the man's cheek and scrape it along his jaw, then she rose and rubbed herself against him so he pulled her between his legs.

Disgust filled him. She was one of the worst. Nellie had been poor and would have had a hard time raising her child, but she still could have done it.

This woman had money enough to hire a damned nanny if she needed to. But she couldn't be bothered to be a mother.

And for that she would pay.

Yes, all the sinners had to suffer.

One by one, he would see that they got what they deserved.

Chapter Six

A cold shiver rippled up Cara's spine as Mason explained the ME's findings.

Just as she'd feared from her preliminary exam, the killer had cut out Nellie's reproductive organs. "This is not a simple murder," she said. "This is a sick man."

Mason grunted in disgust. "You're telling me. He's one of the worst I've seen."

"He obviously has a reason for targeting that specific area."

"Which would make me suspect the baby's father."

"You saw Alfredo," Cara said. "He didn't do this."

Mason raked a hand across his jaw. "I hate to say it but I agree." He drove from the gated community through San Antonio, the lights of the city passing in a blur. "In fact, this M.O. has the markings of a sociopath."

"A sociopath with a cause," Cara said. "A dangerous combination."

Mason nodded, his expression grave. "Damn right it is. It's the stuff serial killers are made of."

Another chill swept over Cara. "So you think he'll kill again?"

"I hope not, but I think so." He hesitated and raked a hand through his shaggy hair. "But a profiler would say that the killer carved out the victim's reproductive organs as some kind of punishment."

"Because she gave birth and allowed her baby to be adopted," Cara surmised.

"Exactly."

Cara's mind raced. Was this killer the same person who'd broken into her clinic? "My God, Mason. What if whoever broke into the clinic wasn't looking for Nellie's baby, but for more victims?"

Mason cursed. "Then we need a list of all the names he may have taken. Those women could be in danger."

"Let's get back to the clinic. I'll look through the files tonight."

Mason grimaced, and they lapsed into silence as he drove back toward the Winchester clinic. A pain clutched Cara's stomach, and she rubbed her belly.

"Are you all right?" Mason asked.

Cara nodded. "I'm just worried about my other patients. If you think they're in danger, we should warn them."

Mason's labored breath echoed in the tense silence. "It's too early for that," he said. "We don't want to create panic until we have more to go on."

Cara accepted his response, but still worry nagged at her.

"Is there something you're not telling me?" Mason asked.

Cara chewed her lip, debating on how much to confess. "I have received some hate mail since I opened the clinic."

He jerked his head toward her. "What kind of hate mail?"

Cara shrugged. "Protests from anonymous sources, people who thought I was starting an abortion clinic."

"But you're not?"

"No," Cara said. "I set up a women's pavilion with OB-GYN care, prenatal and family counseling, and a social worker who helps coordinate adoptions in case single mothers choose that route."

Mason's expression turned stony, but alarm flickered in his eyes. "Were there threats?"

Cara continued to rub her stomach as another Braxton-Hicks contraction assaulted her. "Not anything specifically. Just that I should shut down. Stop encouraging women to give away their children."

Mason hissed. "Dammit, Cara, I need to see those letters."

MASON'S MIND TRAVELED to dark places as he realized the implications of Cara's admission. If someone had sent her threatening letters, then killed one of her patients, Cara might be in danger.

Which meant her child was, as well.

The thought of anyone harming her, much less her baby, made his stomach knot with fear. Dammit, he couldn't let anything happen to her.

His gaze strayed to her hand on her belly again, and protective instincts surged.

Hell, he still didn't know if she was carrying his baby. She might have a boyfriend waiting for her, one who was the baby's father.

He had to know the truth.

She had closed her eyes again, her face riddled with pain.

"When is your baby due?" he asked.

Emotions darkened her face when she looked up at him. "Three weeks."

His mind quickly ticked off that information. Dammit, he could be the father.

The memory of her holding that little girl Lacy taunted him. Cara had looked like a natural mother, loving, caring, tender.

Just the way she was with everyone she knew. Except she would be even more loving with her own child. And she would fight tooth and nail to keep her baby safe.

"Cara," he said, bracing himself for whatever she said. If the baby wasn't his, how would he feel? Relief? Disappointment?

If it was his, what would he do? What would she want him to do?

The answer to that question terrified him.

But he couldn't wait any longer to find out. He

swerved on to a side road, then pulled on to the shoulder.

Cara straightened, alarm on her face. "What are you doing?"

"Are you with someone now?"

Her eyes widened as if that wasn't the question she expected. "No."

"You didn't marry after I left?"

She lifted her head in a defiant gesture. "I don't need a husband to have a child, Mason."

He gestured toward her swollen belly. "Who is the father?"

She gripped the door handle of the car as if she wanted to jump out and run. "I can't believe you're asking me this in the car, especially considering we're in the middle of a murder investigation."

He caught her hand, refusing to let her escape. "Dammit, now is as good a time as any. If someone threatened you because of the clinic and this murder is connected to you, then you and your baby may be in danger."

Panic flickered in her eyes for a brief second before she masked it. "I can take care of myself and my child, Mason. For God's sake, I'm a doctor."

"This has nothing to do with you being a doctor or a competent woman," Mason said, his blood boiling. "It has to do with the fact that a crazed killer murdered one of your patients and may come after you."

His statement must have sunk in, because her face paled in the moonlight spilling through the car. He clenched his hands to keep from pulling her into his arms and comforting her.

She didn't look as if she would welcome his comfort.

"I did the math, Cara. We were together ten months ago. So unless you jumped into bed with another man right after I left—"

"How dare you imply that," Cara seethed.

"Then tell me who the father is."

Cara massaged her stomach again as if to protect the baby inside. "Mason—"

"Just tell me the truth," he said on a pained breath. "Is it mine?"

A long heartbeat passed, then she whispered, "Yes."

RELIEF AND PANIC WARRED inside Cara. As emotions played across Mason's face, she held her breath, unsure whether to expect his temper to explode or for him to shut down completely.

She saw remnants of both, yet a tenderness flashed in his eyes as he laid a hand on her stomach that made tears well in her eyes.

He swallowed twice before he spoke. "Why didn't you tell me?"

Cara averted her gaze, struggling with the memory of how hurt she'd been when he'd left her. "Because you were gone," she said quietly.

"There are telephones," Mason said, a trace of bitterness creeping into his voice.

Cara stiffened. "You made it very clear that you didn't want a relationship," she said. "That you thought mixed marriages didn't work. Granted, I think that's archaic, but it's exactly what you said to me. So what was I supposed to do?" Her own anger shimmied to the surface. "If you didn't want me, why would I think you'd want a child with me?"

He released a heavy sigh. But pain underscored the anger now, making her chest clench.

"I told you how I grew up," he said. "You don't know the half of it, the prejudice, what the kids did to me."

"That was a long time ago," Cara argued. "And I'm sorry for what happened to you, but times have changed."

"Have they?" Mason barked.

Cara's strength rallied. "This is the reason I didn't tell you. That, and I didn't want you to think I was trying to trap you."

"No, you didn't even try to convince me to stay."

Cara gasped as her pride kicked in. "You wanted me to beg you not to leave me? That's not my style."

"No, you're independent, aren't you? You don't need a man."

"No, I don't," Cara said, furious. "I've managed on my own most of my life, and I will continue to do so."

She gestured toward the steering wheel. "Now why don't you drive me to the clinic so I can check those records, then we can go our separate ways for tonight."

And maybe forever.

He could finish the investigation without her.

A dark chuckle reverberated from his chest. "For tonight, maybe," Mason said. "But you're crazy if you think this is over, Cara." He gestured toward her stomach. "That baby is mine, and if he or she is in danger—" He paused. "Do you know if it's a girl or a boy?"

Cara licked her suddenly dry lips. "A boy."

Mason released a shaky sigh. "If my son is in danger, then I'm not letting you out of my sight."

Cara's throat closed. God, no…she couldn't have Mason around smothering her. Worrying about her.

Protecting her.

Making her want him all over again.

She had barely survived the first time he'd left.

MASON SAT FOR A MOMENT digesting their conversation, unable to move or focus on anything except the fact that he was having a son.

With Cara.

The only woman who'd ever made him think twice about settling down. The only woman who stirred his blood with a fever pitch of lust and…other emotions he refused to acknowledge.

Because he was a cop first.

And dammit, he had a serious murder case to

solve. One which involved Cara now more than he'd first realized.

One that potentially jeopardized her life as well as his son's.

His heart raced. Damn. He couldn't let anything happen to them.

"Mason—"

"Don't bother arguing," he said, cutting her off. "Until this maniac is caught, you're going to have to put up with me. After the case is over...then we talk about what to do about our child."

Cara's breath caught, but he ignored her reaction and pulled back into traffic. She might not like it, but he didn't intend to walk away from this baby.

Not like his father had walked away from him.

But what if he's better off without you? Safer?

That thought made his gut constrict.

Nellie Thompson had thought she'd done the right thing by giving her baby to the Davidsons. And they obviously doted on the little girl and would give her a great life. She had been totally unselfish in her choice.

Yet she was dead.

And it was his job to find her killer.

He wouldn't stop until he found justice for the woman and her demented killer was in jail where he belonged.

Cara rested her hands on her stomach as he drove, and he forced himself not to press the issue. They both needed time.

As far as he was concerned, the subject of his involvement was closed.

Traffic had thinned on the country roads, but as he neared the small town, headlights pierced the darkness. He wove through the streets until he reached the Winchester clinic, mentally making a note to call a security company in the morning. Even without this killer on the loose, he couldn't allow her to continue working here with such poor security measures in place.

He parked in front of the clinic and cut the lights. "Let's go in and you can look through the files, then get those letters," he said. "Then I'll follow you home."

"Mason, that's not necessary—"

"Cara," he said quietly. "You don't have to like it, but I will do my job. There is a madman out there who cut out Nellie's reproductive organs. A man who may be after you, so like it or not, I'm your bodyguard."

Emotions flitted across her face, then she seemed to concede but only because she looked exhausted, and he had pointed out the depravity of the killer.

She reached for the door handle, and this time he made it in time to help her out. One touch to her hand, and he felt an immediate connection, a charge of electricity that reminded him of all they had shared.

Cara looked startled for a moment, but she quickly masked it and lumbered toward the door. Jumping into detective mode, he scanned the area in search of trouble, then followed her inside.

The files that had been rifled through still looked scattered, the place dusty from the crime unit. She gathered them up and laid them on the front desk, then flipped through them with a frown.

"What's wrong?"

"I don't see anything missing so far."

Mason scrubbed a hand over his jaw. "Maybe the killer took photos of them or copied files from the computer."

Panic darted in her eyes. "Then he has info on all my patients."

"Don't worry about it now," Mason said, hating the alarm on her face. "For all we know the break-in wasn't related."

Cara didn't look convinced.

"Now find those letters so I can drive you home."

She tucked her hair behind her ear and stood, then walked to her office in the back.

Mason followed, his instincts on alert.

She unlocked a safe then removed a manila envelope from the inside.

"You saved them all?" he asked.

She nodded. "I thought I might need them, just in case there was trouble."

"Smart thinking." He took them from her, then helped her up from the chair. The fact that she didn't protest told him she must be totally exhausted, or frightened, or in pain.

Or all three.

His lungs squeezed for air as they walked outside. She settled inside her Pathfinder, then drove from town, and he followed, his heart in his throat.

The image of Nellie's mangled body taunted him.

Lord help him, he'd die before he'd let that happen to Cara, or allow anyone to hurt his son.

HE TRACED A FINGER down her slender throat, smiling at how easily she'd fallen for his charms. Of course, the alcohol she'd consumed had blurred her mind, but that had been her choice.

Not his.

He had been watching her for a week now and partying was an every night outing for her.

Tonight would be her last.

"Come here, lover boy," she whispered against his neck.

The cheap motel lights glittered outside, blinking against the dingy sheers covering the window. Country music from the bar next door blared through the parking lot, echoing through the thin walls of the room and pulsing around them in a sickening thud.

That music would drown out her screams.

He smiled again, then slid the knife from his pocket and rose above her. She raked her fingers over his shirt and popped the buttons.

Disgust rose in his throat.

He refused to dirty himself with her filthy body. Instead when she thought he was going to screw her, he jammed the knife into her belly and twisted it. Her scream pierced the air, lost in the wailing sound of the music.

Then blood spurted onto his hands and relief filled him. One more sinner had died for her sins.

Now on to another...

Chapter Seven

Mason clenched his jaw as he followed Cara across the BBL to her cabin. He was staying a couple of cabins over while he was here and had no idea how close he'd been to her.

If he had, would he have made an effort to see her?

No, he probably would have avoided her. Seeing her and not having her was just too damn hard.

When he'd first heard of the BBL, he'd known he had to join the group of ranchers who devoted time and money to help troubled boys. God knows he would have ended up nowhere if the men on the reservation hadn't taken him under their wing. They had not only taught him how to hunt and fish, how to utilize tracking skills, but had also instilled a pride for his people and a tolerance for other nationalities.

The one golden rule—they had a zero tolerance policy against hurting women or children.

Night had set in, darkness bathing the ranch, the sound of night critters chirping and scrambling through the wooded areas echoing through the evening air. The campers had turned in by now, the camp counselors planning the next day's events.

The image of the boys he'd met flashed in his mind. Their stories were all different yet held similarities that bonded them to this place. Broken families, abuse, crime, poverty, orphans...

A couple of the stories had broken his heart. TJ was six, had been in and out of the hospital because his father had beaten him so badly that now he walked with a limp and was skittish about getting close to anyone. Micky's mother had left him in charge of his two younger brothers when he was only five. Finally when a neighbor caught the little guy stealing food from her pantry, she realized they had been left alone for almost a month. The mother had later been found dead in a crack house.

And little Deagan's father had left him in a garbage can at two months after his wife had walked out.

He raked his hand over his chin. God, he'd never thought about being a father before, but there was no way he would walk out on his own kid.

He knew the pain that caused. The feeling of betrayal, of shame, of guilt and abandonment. Hadn't he asked himself a thousand times why his father hadn't loved him?

He'd assumed his mixed heritage was the reason, but deep down he'd believed he wasn't...lovable.

He'd never let his kid think that.

Cara turned on to the road leading to the south end cabins, and they bypassed the area where Nellie's car and body had been found. The image of Nellie's stomach cut open haunted him.

Had she been on her way to see Cara? Had the killer known where she was going?

That thought sent a bolt of fear straight through him.

What if he was waiting on her now?

CARA'S NERVES WERE on edge as she parked in front of her cabin. It had been a long day.

First she'd spent time at the clinic at the ranch, then at the Winchester clinic in town, then that horrible phone call about Nellie. Her back was aching, and she rubbed it as she grabbed her purse and hauled herself from the car.

Mason's headlights loomed behind her as he rolled to a stop, and she fought the urge to rush inside and close the door, shutting him out.

Tonight had been too emotional. Nellie's death. The clinic had been broken into.

And she'd finally been forced to tell the father of her child about their baby.

Fatigue clawed at her, but she gathered the last remnants of her pride and strength and walked up the porch steps. She had to make sure Mason knew she wasn't trying to trap him into playing father.

Or husband to her.

That she would and could stand on her own.

The sound of Mason's car door slamming echoed behind her, then his boots crunched gravel and pounded the wood boards as he climbed the steps. She felt his big body behind her, and his ominous presence tempted her to lean into him.

She was so tired tonight, so shaken by all that had happened, so drawn to him just as she had been when she'd first met him, that she wanted to fall into his arms and have him hold her and assure her everything would be all right.

But that was a fantasy, not reality, and she lived in the real world. Not only did she have to protect herself, she had to protect her son.

The keys jangled in her hand as she fumbled to unlock the door. Mason took them, then unlocked it for her.

"Thanks." Cara turned to him, determined he leave before he stepped inside her space. Having him in her cabin, leaving his scent, his image in the rooms where she found solace, would only make her miss him more when he left.

"Cara, I was thinking," Mason said. "If Nellie was coming to see you, her killer might know where you live."

Cara sighed, too weary to contemplate his comment. "It's been two days since he killed her, Mason. If he was coming after me, he would have done so by now."

Mason's face constricted. "We can't be sure of that, Cara. He might have come to the clinic looking for you, got angry when you weren't there and trashed the place in his rage."

She shivered at the thought. "Thanks for following me home, Mason, but I'm tired. I just want to go to bed."

A tense heartbeat passed between them, riddled with what she'd said. Her mind strayed to images of him following her, climbing into bed with her, holding her all night.

A second later, reality hit her with the force of another Braxton Hicks contraction. For goodness' sakes, she was nine months pregnant, not exactly sexy. No man wanted to crawl in bed with a woman when she looked like a whale.

Besides, they had too much to discuss to even think about getting close and personal again.

Mason put a hand on the door to keep her from closing it. "Let me at least check out the cabin."

Cara knew Mason well enough not to bother arguing. He hadn't wanted a commitment with her, but he was totally committed to his job and took protecting others seriously.

She gestured for him to go in. "Fine, suit yourself."

His gaze met hers as he brushed past her, the heat simmering between them igniting fantasies of smoldering kisses and wanton touches.

She banished them immediately. Those thoughts had gotten her pregnant in the first place.

She had no room for them in her life now.

Mason felt Cara's belly brush his stomach as he inched past her, and his pulse jumped. Normally a pregnant woman's body wasn't a turn on, but this was Cara and she was round with his child.

The realization that his little boy was growing inside her made him pause, and he was tempted to lay his hand on her belly. To feel his son move inside her.

But Cara sucked in a breath and took a step back, a warning in her eyes.

Dammit. She didn't want him in her life. That was obvious.

And she didn't particularly want him in their baby's life, either. If she had, she would have let him know about the pregnancy. That story about not wanting to trap him was just a cover to mask the fact that she was independent and hadn't cared when he'd left before.

After all, she hadn't exactly begged him to stay or declared her love.

He forced himself past her; he had to focus on the job and that meant making sure the demented man who'd butchered Nellie hadn't come here for Cara.

Senses honed, he reached for his weapon, held it at the ready, then flipped on a light and scanned the living room. Most of the cabins on the ranch were built in a similar design with a spacious living room/kitchen combination, bed and bath. Rustic logs comprised the walls and floors, which were decorated with hand-woven Native American blankets, and baskets as well as photographs of the Texas landscape. There were both one bedroom and two bedroom units, depending on the employee's needs.

The living room and kitchen were empty, a blanket folded neatly over the camel colored sofa, a few medical magazines stacked on the rustic coffee table along with mothering, baby and parenting ones.

He paused to listen, but the cabin was quiet. A good sign.

He moved to the right and noted the master bedroom. Cara's was a four-poster pine Shaker style with a crocheted canopy. He inched into the room, noted it was also empty and so was the adjoining bath.

Satisfied there wasn't an intruder in her bedroom, he checked the second bedroom. His heart sputtered at the sight of the crib. Cara had painted the room a soft blue and had added touches of Native American artwork on the walls. A handwoven basket that looked as if it had come from the reservation held baby blankets, another one held diapers and baby supplies, and a rug with horses woven into it covered the center of the floor.

He immediately pictured Cara in the rocking chair in the corner, cradling their son in her arms as she nursed him and sang lullabies.

The room was just waiting for her to bring the baby home.

Yet she'd planned to give birth and raise the child without ever telling him.

Anger pummeled him, and he fisted his hands. He wanted to shake her and demand to know how she could make that decision for him.

What would she have told his son about him? That he hadn't cared? That he hadn't wanted him?

The sound of her footsteps made him jerk his gaze toward her. The soft light from the living room spilled across her face, and their gazes locked. For a moment, he couldn't breathe.

He was so angry with her that he had to grit his teeth to keep from lashing out.

Yet, she looked so damn radiant standing in the dim light with her rounded frame that he wanted to sweep her into his arms and make love to her.

"The house is clear, Mason," Cara said, her voice tight. "Please leave now so I can rest."

Dammit, he wanted to push her for answers, make her admit that she did need him. Make her see that even if he hadn't wanted marriage, that he would do right by their son.

But fatigue lined her face, and he realized the day had worn on her. He couldn't make things worse by pressuring her.

"Fine. I'll look at those letters tonight then send them to forensics." Forcing himself not to touch her as he passed, he headed to the door. She followed him to lock up, and he turned back once he was on the porch.

"Call me if you need anything."

She gave a clipped nod, but stubbornness had settled back in her eyes. So he left without another word.

Still, he waited in his car until he saw her lock up, then he drove to his cabin. He gathered the envelope of letters Cara had given him, then hurried inside his own cabin.

His stomach growled, so he heated a pizza from the freezer, popped open a beer and sat down to study the hate mail.

Several letters looked as if they had come from the same source. Antiabortion activists, a church group, then a few individuals urging single mothers to keep their unborn children. The common thread—they accused Cara of encouraging mothers to abandon their children instead of taking responsibility for their babies.

His suspicions mounted as the warnings became more sinister. One specifically caught his eye. The words had been cut from newspapers and magazines.

"Close the clinic or you'll be sorry."

Had the man who'd murdered Nellie sent it because Cara hadn't listened?

CARA STEEPED A CUP OF TEA and made toast, then decided she should feed her baby something substantial so she heated some soup.

By the time she finished, her back was throbbing so she ran a bath, carried a second cup of tea with her into the bathroom, shut the door and climbed in the tub. The warm water felt heavenly, and she leaned back and closed her eyes, struggling with her emotions.

When she'd seen Mason standing at the edge of the baby's room, she'd wondered what he'd thought.

He had looked so huge and gruff next to those tiny baby things.

Yet oddly, she imagined him holding their little boy and it seemed…right.

A sound from the other room jarred her eyes open, and she sat up with a frown. Had Mason returned?

She listened for a second longer, her nerves prickling. Today she'd seen Nellie's brutalized body in the ground. Although the image haunted her, she willed it away. Still, she couldn't forget that Nellie had been murdered, and that the killer was at large.

Shivering, she stood, grabbed a towel and dried off. She slipped on her warm flannel gown, then hung up her towel and stepped into the hallway.

The moment she did, the wind whistled through the house, rattling the windows.

A cold chill enveloped her, and she froze, instantly scanning the living area from her vantage point. Then she realized the chill was coming from her bedroom.

A tremble started deep inside her, and she grabbed a can of hairspray from the bathroom as a weapon, holding it in front of her as she turned the corner and flipped on the light.

Someone had been in her room.

The window stood open, the curtain flapping in the breeze. Then her gaze fell to her bed and she gasped.

A small box lay on top of the coverlet, a note placed on top.

She scanned the room again as she inched close enough to read the message.

"Bad mothers are sinners. Sinners must die."

Her stomach revolted at the meaning, then bile rose to her throat.

The note had been written in blood.

Chapter Eight

Cara struggled for a breath. Dear God, was that human blood?

The note hadn't been there when Mason had checked earlier, meaning someone had been inside her cabin.

Only moments ago while she was in the bath.

They could still be nearby watching her.

Her hand shook as she raced to her purse and grabbed her phone. She called Mason's number, then hurried to shut the window. The cool air sent another chill through her, and she peered through the window, searching for the intruder while the phone rang.

A shadow moved at the edge of the woods, headlights flickering in the distance. The phone rang again, then a click and Mason answered.

"Cara?"

"Someone was in my cabin while I was in the bath."

His breath rushed out. "What?"

"He's gone now but he left a note."

"I'm on my way." The phone went dead and Cara quickly pulled on a robe, then went to the front door to watch for Mason.

MASON'S HEART POUNDED as he grabbed his gun and raced to his car. Dammit, he'd checked Cara's cabin earlier and it had been clean.

But the intruder must have been watching. Waiting on him to leave Cara alone.

He floored the gas and sped across the terrain, lights beaming across grass and gravel. He scanned the property as he drove, looking for anything suspicious, a car or truck driving too fast, escaping.

The ranch seemed quiet though, the sound of a lone coyote howling in the distance. Brody had had trouble on the ranch before, and had hired extra security then. Mason made a mental note to make sure he still had that security in place.

Better yet, he'd stay with Cara. No way he'd leave her alone and vulnerable.

He slowed, easing near her cabin, eyes darting around the edges of the property to all the places a killer could hide. Something moved near the right corner, and he tensed. But a second later, he realized it was a stray dog.

He threw the car into Park, jumped out and stalked up the steps. Cara must have been watching for him because she swung the door open. She looked pale and shaken, and dammit, she was about to burst with his child.

He couldn't resist. He pulled her up against him. The fact that she didn't push him away indicated just how upset she was. "Are you okay?"

She nodded against him, her breathing unsteady.

Her fear twisted his insides, and he held her for a moment, soothing her with soft whispers. Finally she relaxed, her breathing steadying.

But he sensed the moment she realized she'd allowed herself to lean on him, and she pulled away.

"What happened?" he asked, missing the contact.

"I locked up after you left, then ate a bite. While I was in the bath, I thought I heard something." She knotted the belt around her robe. "When I came out, the bedroom window was open. Then I saw the note."

"Note?"

"Yes," Cara said, fear flickering in her eyes. "He left a note and a box."

"What's inside the box?"

'I haven't opened it yet," Cara said with a shiver. "But the note…it's disturbing."

Mason strode to the bedroom, then halted by the bed. Dammit. Now he understood what had upset Cara so badly—the words had been written in blood.

"Do you think it's human blood?" Cara asked.

"I don't know, but I'll send it to forensics and find out." He leaned closer to inspect it, his stomach churning as his mind raced to a dark place.

If the blood was human, did it belong to Nellie Thompson?

"Did you touch it?" Mason asked.

"No, God no," Cara whispered.

"Good. Let me get a kit from the car. I don't want to contaminate the evidence."

Cara nodded, and he rushed outside then returned a moment later with his crime kit. He pulled on latex gloves, then bagged the note. Had it been left by the same person who'd sent that threatening note to the clinic?

Anger immediately hit him as he opened the wooden box.

Cara peered over his shoulder. "What is it?"

"A deerskin pouch," Mason said.

"I don't understand," Cara said with a frown.

Unfortunately he did. "It's called a navel fetish. It's actually a birth amulet."

"Like a gift the mother receives when she delivers?"

"Not exactly. It's used by Native Americans for holding an umbilical cord. In the Plains tradition, the mother places the pouch on the cradleboard above the baby's head. At a later age, the child wears it around his neck or attached to clothing. The amulet brings the baby good luck and keeps the umbilical cord preserved, and the mother-child connection alive."

Cara clasped her hands together. "Is anything inside it?"

Mason clenched his jaw and peeked inside. "No, it's empty."

He glanced at Cara and saw the significance of its meaning sink in. "He left it to me because he believes I'm breaking that mother-child connection."

Mason wanted to deny her comment, but he couldn't.

Coupled with the Thompson woman's murder, the threatening notes Cara had received at the clinic, and the fact that someone had broken in and left this pouch, he had to conclude that they were all connected.

Which meant that Cara and his baby were definitely in danger.

"YOU THINK THE PERSON who left this is the same one who killed Nellie?" Cara asked.

"Yes." Mason's gaze met hers. "It also makes me think that he may come after you, Cara."

Cara fiddled with the belt to her robe, averting her eyes. "We don't know that, Mason. In fact, the killer could have randomly chosen Nellie."

Mason grunted. "You don't believe that and neither do I."

Cara sank onto the edge of the bed, her stomach churning. "Dear Lord, I hope you're wrong."

"So do I, but I examined those letters you received, and there are a couple that sound threatening."

She massaged her lower back. "I can't believe this is happening. All I wanted to do was to help the women around here."

"And you are helping them," Mason said. "It's not your fault some sicko targeted you."

Cara wanted to believe him, but guilt nagged at her. "But he blames me. He thinks I'm destroying families."

"He's a sick man," Mason said in a low voice. "He was probably abandoned as a child or his mother gave him up, so now he's generalized his rage to all mothers who choose adoption."

Her gaze swung to his, and a sliver of anger flashed in her eyes. "I don't tell the women what to do, I only provide counseling to help them cope with their situations."

"What about our baby?" Mason asked in a deep voice. "You're not planning to give our son to someone else to raise, are you?"

Cara stood, her own temper rising. "No, Mason, I fully intend to raise this child on my own."

Mason stepped closer, so close his breath bathed her face.

"The hell you are. That baby is *my* son. I don't intend for him to think that I ran out on him like my old man did."

An electric charge simmered between them, taut with tension and memories.

And the heat that had drawn her to him in the first place.

She was too exhausted, too frightened, too upset about Nellie to deal with this. "Mason, I can't talk about it right now. I… All I can think about is Nellie and catching this maniac before he hurts some-one else."

Mason's gaze remained on her for a heartbeat, then fell to her belly. The baby chose that moment to kick again, hard enough for her to wince, and Mason laid his hand on her stomach.

Cara sucked in a sharp breath at the contact, her heart squeezing at the emotions playing across his face as he felt their son move.

The first time she'd felt that tiny little flutter, she'd been humbled and awed by the realization that a tiny life was growing inside her. She'd imagined a little boy, one with big dark eyes and dark hair like his father.

Love had swelled within her, overflowing and rousing protective instincts stronger than anything she'd ever felt before.

Those same emotions were mirrored in Mason's face now.

"Cara—"

"Please," she whispered, choking back the temp-tation to rush into his arms. "Please let's just find Nellie's killer and then we'll talk."

Mason's jaw tightened, his breath hissing out be-tween clenched teeth, but he nodded in silent agree-ment.

"I'll send all this to the lab in the morning. For now, go get some rest."

"Thanks." Cara started toward the door to see him out, but he stood stone still.

"I'm not leaving you here tonight," Mason said in a tone that brooked no argument. "Not knowing that the man who killed Nellie might have been in your house."

The reminder sent a shudder through her. But she didn't know if she could sleep with Mason so close by, either.

"Go on to bed," he said. "I'll take the couch."

Grateful for the reprieve from the discussion about their son, she hurried to the bedroom, then shut the door.

But as she crawled into bed, the image of that navel fetish and Nellie's face taunted her. And it was all she could do not to get up and beg Mason to come to bed with her.

MASON WATCHED THE DOOR close and gritted his teeth. As much as he wanted to join Cara, he couldn't.

He had to force his mind back on the case.

Getting distracted by his personal feelings might mean Cara's life.

That is, if they were dealing with a repeat offender. His gut instinct told him it was only a matter of time before they found another body.

That whoever had killed her had left this navel fetish to make a point. He wanted the Winchester Clinic shut down, and he would kill to get his message across.

Mason had to stop him before the bastard took any more lives.

He phoned Sheriff McRae to fill him in. "I'm sending this note and the navel fetish to the lab in the morning. I also have letters Cara received that I want the lab to analyze."

"You think he may come after Dr. Winchester?" Sheriff McRae asked.

Fear clutched Mason's chest. "Yes. But at this point, he may be trying to punish her by making her watch other women die."

He hung up, his head reeling. This madman wanted to make Cara feel guilty for the other women's deaths.

Torment was his game of lust.

Dammit, he would find the SOB and lock him up forever.

He would not let him hurt Cara or his child.

HE LIT THE COALS inside the sweat hut, then stood at the top of the boulder and looked across at the plains. His father had taught him about the ways of the Natives while his mother had been nothing but a cheating whore.

He grasped onto the values of the Comanches, closed his eyes and willed the gods to hear his pleas to save the mothers who selfishly sinned and coveted their own pleasures instead of their God-given task of protecting and taking care of their young.

The blood from the woman he'd freed from sin tonight still stained his skin, but he dipped his fingers into the icy stream, washing the blood away.

The crimson color mingled with the clear saintly water and flowed downstream.

The blood had been washed away just as her sins had when he'd bled them from her tainted soul.

A peaceful feeling overcame him as he imagined Dr. Winchester finding the amulet he'd left for her. She was an instrument for evil.

And she had to be stopped.

But she had to be punished first.

Taking solace from the fact that he'd finally begun his mission, he stripped his clothes, laid them on the rocks and stepped inside the sweat hut.

Now he would cleanse himself and prepare for the next sinner.

Chapter Nine

Cara finally fell into a fitful sleep. But in her dreams she was running from a madman.

He waved a knife in the air, its shiny glint flickering against the darkness.

His face was shrouded in the night, his growl an animal-like sound as he bellowed her name.

A spasm of pain shot through her belly, and she clutched her stomach, the pressure of the contraction nearly bringing her to her knees. But she couldn't stop.

She had to keep running. Had to save her baby.

She suddenly tripped over a group of rocks, then plowed to the ground. A scream caught in her throat when she saw that she'd landed on top of Nellie Thompson's body.

"I've got you now," he snarled. "You'll pay for your sins."

She screamed and tried to push up, but her hand touched the cold stiffness of Nellie's skin, and horror rippled through her. Still, she clawed at the ground, dirt sifting through her fingers as she rolled herself away.

He lunged toward her and grabbed her arm, but she twisted and fought him, desperate to pull herself up and escape. But her bulk made it too difficult and another pain seized her.

Dear God, the baby was coming!

She screamed for help, trying to shove him off with her feet, but he lunged toward her and sank the knife into her chest. Pain overcame her, and she gasped for air as blood spilled from her.

Then he lowered the knife and carved out her belly. She heard the sound of her baby crying, then watched helplessly as he lifted her child in his arms.

Cara jerked awake with a cry, trembling all over.

Suddenly the door swung open and Mason was there, leaning over her, touching her, pulling her up against him.

"Shh, it was just a nightmare," he whispered against her hair.

Cara struggled to shake the terror from her soul. "But it seemed so real."

"What did you dream?"

"That Nellie's killer was after me," Cara said. "That I fell into her grave and he took my baby."

A shudder coursed through her. It had been a nightmare.

But there was truth in it, as well. If Mason was right about this maniac targeting her, eventually he might try to kill her and take her son.

MASON HATED THE FEAR in Cara's voice.

Unfortunately she had a right to be afraid. Hopefully that fear would force her to be cautious and keep her alive.

The thought of anything happening to her and his son sent terror through him, and he wrapped his arms around her and held her tighter. "I'm not going to let him get to you," Mason said. "I promise you, Cara. I'll find the bastard and lock him away so he can't hurt you or our baby."

She clung to his arms, her breathing finally steadying. "I'll look through my files today and see if anyone seems suspicious."

"Good." He glanced at the window where early morning light streamed through the sheers. At least Cara had slept a few hours.

He had been stone cold awake, too afraid to sleep for fear her intruder might return.

"I need to run the note and amulet to the lab. I called Brody last night and caught him up to speed."

"Does he want me to leave the ranch?"

"No, he's alerting his security team to watch out for trouble. But I think you should go with me."

"I have patients to see today," Cara said.

"Maybe you should shut down the clinic until we find out if this maniac is targeting you and your patients," Mason suggested.

"I can't do that," Cara said. "Those women need me. Besides, I have two patients, young girls, about to deliver. I need to check on them."

Mason reluctantly released her and pulled away. "Stay here until I can run to the lab, then I'll drive you to the clinic."

Cara shook her head. "No, go. I promised Brody I'd stop by the center here first."

"Then wait here until I return. I'll arrange for security to be installed at the clinic on my way to the lab." He stood then pulled a backup pistol he had in his car and laid it on the end table. "Keep that just in case."

"I took an oath to save lives, Mason, not take them."

"I know you did." Mason made a point to glance at her stomach. "But you're also carrying a baby who is depending on you to protect him."

Cara's face blanched, then she closed her eyes as if to gain her composure, and when she opened them, he saw acceptance in her eyes.

If the psycho who butchered Nellie tried to hurt their baby, she would defend him with every fiber of her being.

Mason headed back to his place to shower. An hour later, he logged the evidence from Cara's into the lab and met with the forensic expert, Jody Tyler.

"What is that?" Jody asked when he showed her the amulet.

Mason explained the Plains tradition and the ME's report. "Did you find any forensics or prints on her body or at her place?"

"I'm afraid not."

"Can you tell what kind of weapon was used to kill her?"

"Yes." She led him to a computer with a screen shot of various knives. "Judging from the size of the blade, and the width of the knife wound, I'd say he used a hunting knife, one like this."

Mason frowned, studying the knife.

"It's a large buffalo skinner," Jody began.

"I recognize it. Handle is made from hardwood, blade ten-inch carbon steel, sharp enough to skin an animal and strong enough to cut through bone."

Jody nodded. "Unfortunately it's not uncommon. Several websites offer it for sale."

Mason's stomach lurched at the thought of a man using it on a woman. "The shops in Texas that sell Native American arts and crafts and gear also carry them."

"True. But if you find the weapon, it probably has a serial number on it that might help us trace the buyer."

Mason had another idea. "I'll check with a friend at the reservation who specializes in making knives." He might have sold one to a customer that roused suspicion.

"We also found a message on the victim's phone that you need to hear," Jody said.

Mason gritted his teeth as she played the voice mail. "Do you know where your baby is?"

Dammit, it was the same message Nellie had received in the mail. Which meant she had definitely had a stalker.

Was he hunting for another victim now?

CARA PHONED SHERESE as soon as Mason left to give her a heads-up on the break-in at the clinic. "Mason is sending a security team over to install a security system and cameras today. I'll be there in a little while."

"Okay. I called Nacona in and he cleaned already. But are you sure we shouldn't shut down for the day?"

"You know I can't do that, Sherese. Betina and Connie are coming in this morning. They're too close to delivery for me to miss their appointments." Cara paused. "But if you're too nervous to be there, I understand. You have your own family to think of."

Sherese gave a soft laugh. "Don't worry about me, Doc. I've dealt with worse than a druggie looking for a fix."

Cara rubbed her forehead. "I wish that's all it was."

"You think it was something else?" Sherese asked, alarmed.

"It could be someone targeting me," Cara said.

"Then you need to be careful, Cara. You have a family on the way, too."

"I know," Cara said. "Mason is coming with me."

"Mason?" Sherese asked, a sliver of shock in her voice. "You mean Mason, as in the baby's father?"

"Yes," Cara said. "And yes, he knows the baby is his now."

"Oh, my," Sherese said softly. "How did that go?"

"About like you'd expect. He was surprised, angry…but I can't worry about that. We have to find out who killed Nellie. I'm terrified he may target someone else from the clinic."

"Then we should warn the patients," Sherese said.

Cara clenched her jaw. "Mason thinks it's too soon to do that. But if something else happens, I'll insist that we do." She hesitated. "My phone's buzzing. I'll see you in a couple of hours." Cara switched to take the incoming call.

"Cara, it's Brody. Mason filled me in. Are you all right?"

"Yes."

"I hate to ask this, but we have a couple of kids who need to be looked at."

"I'll be there in five." Cara finished dressing, grabbed her medical bag and hurried to her Pathfinder. Grateful for something to distract her from her own problems, she embraced the kids waiting on her at the BBL clinic.

"Let's see what we have here, guys."

Keith was six and coughing, so she listened to

his chest, checked his throat and ears. "Looks like a case of tonsillitis," she said. "A little antibiotic and you'll feel better soon."

"I don't wanna miss riding lessons," he said, his voice hoarse.

Cara ruffled his hair. "Don't worry, you won't." She gave him a hug, retrieved the sample antibiotics she kept to give to his camp leader, then met ten-year-old Rueben. "What's going on, Rueben?"

"My ankle hurts." The poor kid was way too skinny and fragile for a boy his age.

"Let me take a look." He climbed on the exam table, and she pulled off his shoe and sock. His ankle was slightly swollen, and she twisted and pressed in various spots, then took an X-ray. A few minutes later, she showed it to him. "Good news, kiddo. It's not broken, just a slight sprain."

His big eyes widened with panic. "I have to leave camp?"

"No, we'll wrap it, and you take it easy for a day or two, then you'll be back to normal."

He grinned, and her heart broke at the sight of his teeth. She made a mental note to arrange for a dentist to offer services at the BBL as soon as possible.

She finished up with some routine checks for colds, then looked up to find Mason watching her.

"Are you ready?" he asked.

She nodded. "Any news?"

Mason led her out to his car, and they settled inside before he spoke. "Forensics found a message on

Nellie's phone. It was similar to the note we found in her house."

Cara's heart pounded. "So she was worried about her baby?"

"It looks that way. She was probably on her way to see you when he killed her."

Cara's throat swelled. So Nellie had been killed because of her...

MASON DROVE CARA to the clinic and waited while she saw her morning patients, two young single women who looked like they were going to deliver any day.

He introduced himself to Cara's assistant Sherese, an olive-skinned woman with striking dark hair and brown eyes.

"Cara explained about the break-in and Nellie Thompson's murder?"

Sherese nodded. "I hated to hear about that. Poor woman." She sorted through a stack of files. "But the baby is safe?"

"Yes," Mason said. "It doesn't look like the killer murdered her to get the child. But he had been watching her, stalking her."

"Lord help us all," Sherese said. "Nobody seems safe these days."

"Can you think of anyone who's been here, maybe an expectant father, disgruntled spouse or ex-husband, someone with issues against the women's clinic?"

Sherese fiddled with her long braid. "Hmm, there was a man who came in pushing religious fliers on us. Seemed kind of fanatical."

"Do you still have one of those fliers?"

She scrunched her mouth in thought. "I think I threw them out." She stood and walked over to a bulletin board where they'd posted information on support groups for single mothers, dates for free vaccinations for children, along with fliers on child care workers and programs for young children. Then she reached into the trash and removed a white paper emblazoned with information on a local religious group and their meeting place.

A man named Reverend Webber Parch led the group.

"Thanks, Sherese, I'll check this guy out."

Cara emerged from the back, her arm around a young teenager who looked nervous. "Call me if you start having contractions," Cara said.

The young woman put her hand on Cara's belly. "What if you go first, Doc?"

Cara laughed softly. "Then Sadie Whitefeather will deliver your baby."

The young girl relaxed, then left, and Cara greeted a Native American girl clutching her boyfriend's hands. The boy seemed to be doting on the girl. Mason grimaced, wondering if that love would last once the child arrived.

His cell phone buzzed, and he checked the screen,

a bad feeling crawling up his spine when he saw the sheriff's number. "Blackpaw here."

"It's Sheriff McRae. I hate to tell you this, Blackpaw, but we have another body."

Mason's chest clenched. Dammit to hell.

It was true. They had a serial killer on their hands.

Chapter Ten

"Where are you?" Mason asked the sheriff.

"Out at the landfill on Old Coal Road."

Mason gritted his teeth. "You think it's the same killer?"

"Yes," Sheriff McRae said. "He covered the grave in stones just like before."

"Who found her?"

"Couple of teenagers who were scavenging the dump. They saw a stray dog pawing at the ground. Damn dog dug up just enough for them to see there was a body."

Sheriff McRae made a disgusted sound low in his throat. "I already called a crime unit."

"Have you identified her?"

"Not yet."

"All right, I'm on my way." He stowed his phone on his belt, then explained what happened to Sherese.

Sherese headed toward the exam rooms. "I'll tell Cara."

He glanced at the flier again while he waited on

her to return. Cara and the pregnant teen and her boyfriend emerged from the back. Cara's face was strained, although she tried to hide it from her patients.

"Everything looks good. You have a couple more weeks to go, but call me if anything changes."

The teenage father looked up at Cara sheepishly. He was trying so hard to be a man. "Thank you, Dr. Winchester. You take good care of my little one."

Cara patted his back. "You're both going to do fine," she assured them.

The couple left together, holding hands.

"Sherese said there was another victim," Cara said as soon as the couple disappeared out the door.

Mason nodded. "I just talked to the sheriff."

"How can you be sure it's the same guy?"

"I can't until we look at the scene and the victim, but he buried her in the same Comanche ritualistic manner."

Anguish flickered across Cara's face. "Let me get my bag and I'll go with you." She disappeared down the hall.

Mason wanted to shield her from the sight of another murder, but he couldn't do that. She was a doctor, the assistant coroner for God's sake, and too entrenched in the investigation for him to hold back.

Besides, if he'd even suggested it, she would have balked.

Sherese shifted, obviously anxious. "You have to find this creep, Detective Blackpaw."

"I will," Mason promised.

Although how many more women would die before he did?

CARA AND MASON lapsed into a strained silence, both lost in worry over the case as they drove toward the dump. By the time they arrived at the dump on the country road, her nerves were completely frayed.

The stench of the landfill clogged the air as they climbed out, and Cara paused to catch her breath while Mason retrieved his crime kit.

"You don't have to do this," Mason said, his voice gruff.

"Yes, I do." Cara lifted her medical bag from the car, then forged ahead, leading the way to the sheriff's car.

"Where are the kids who found her?" Mason asked.

"They were pretty shook up, so one boy's father picked them up."

"They were clean?" Mason asked.

The sheriff nodded. "Just a couple of adolescents," McRae said. "Father assured me they're good students. They had a science project, something about recycled products. That's why they came here. I have their contact information in case we need to follow up."

"They didn't see anyone?" Mason asked.

"Naw. And we haven't dug her up yet," McRae said. "Waiting on you and the crime lab to do that."

Cara spotted the mound of dirt and stones and paused.

For a moment, the cruelty of the killer's disregard for the woman's life, and her death, immobilized her. The poor woman's eyes and forehead had been exposed, but the rest of her body was still underground.

She glanced around the landfill, a chill engulfing her at the stench and piles of trash and garbage. "This is…even more vile," she said. "Why bury her out here in this pit?"

"Because he saw her as trash," Mason suggested.

Cara frowned. "It's different from Nellie."

"Yet the same," Mason said. "It's almost as if he didn't care if this woman wasn't found."

"Like she didn't deserve our attention," Cara said, repulsed by the killer's lack of respect for another human.

"Yet he still used the stones when he could have just left her here," Mason added, as if that fact perplexed him.

"Which means this ritual is important to him," Cara interjected. "It's so ingrained in his belief system that even if he wanted to discard her body differently, he couldn't do that or he'd defy his own faith."

Mason began to snap pictures while Cara snapped a few of her own. By then the crime unit arrived. They photographed the grave site, then Mason worked with one of the techs and the sheriff to comb the area for forensics. The problem was that there was so much territory and junk along with tire prints from garbage trucks that it would be hard to pinpoint anything out of place.

Cara donned latex gloves, and she and the second crime tech brushed the dirt away to reveal the woman's face. Cara prayed she wasn't one of her patients, but as soon as the tech exposed her hair, she knew her prayers had gone unanswered.

The woman's name was Yolanda Farraday. She had brought a baby boy into the world two months ago and then given him up for adoption because she was terminally ill.

Tears filled her eyes.

Had the man who'd killed her known that she was sick?

Or had he assumed she just hadn't wanted her child?

MASON CURSED AS HE scanned the area near the grave site. The son of a bitch had to know that burying the victim here would make finding any evidence nearly impossible.

Which was probably another reason he chose the spot.

He found a button near the grave and bagged it. It looked like it came off a military jacket, but had a feeling it would be a dead end. The button could easily have come from the trash pile.

"This is a nightmare," the crime tech said. "Like a needle in a haystack."

Mason squinted as the Texas sun shimmered off the metal in the trash pile. The temperature was rising which would only make the stench intensify as the day wore on.

"Hell, we didn't turn up anything that would help us at the first crime scene. No surprise if he was just as careful here."

"I'll take another look around," the crime tech said.

"Look for any signs of a navel fetish," Mason told him. Although he hadn't left one with the first victim—he'd given that gift to Cara.

Antsy to check on her, he handed the button off to the crime tech to log into evidence, then returned to the grave site. Cara's skin looked ashen as she leaned over the grave.

"Cara?"

She glanced up at him from where she was kneeling on the ground, and he saw the victim's face, deathly white, covered in dirt, her hair a stringy mess, tangled in the soil.

"Do you know her?" he asked, half praying she didn't, that he was wrong and that this case didn't revolve around her and the clinic.

But pain flashed in her eyes and she nodded. "Her name is Yolanda Farraday. She's thirty-four."

"Her injuries?"

"The same as Nellie," Cara said in a gravelly voice.

Damn sick bastard.

Cara pushed to her feet, swaying slightly, and he caught her. "Do you need to sit down?"

She shook her head. "It's not fair, Mason, it's just not right."

He swallowed back his own disgust. Worry for her superseded anything else. "I know."

Cara gestured toward the body. "No, you don't. The way he left her here, it's not right."

"Of course it's not right," he said, anger lacing his voice. "He's a maniac."

"But if he's mad at these women for giving their children up for adoption, he should learn the whole damn story." She walked to the edge of the landfill near a cluster of trees and leaned over as if she had to get some air.

He didn't blame her. Between the putrid odors of the landfill and the dead body, his own stomach was churning.

Concerned about her and the baby, he strode over to her. "Cara?"

A low sob ripped from her throat. "Yolanda did agree for another couple to adopt her child, but it wasn't because she didn't want her baby."

Mason frowned. He understood that sometimes people felt trapped in their circumstances whether it was poverty, lack of education, an abusive relationship. "What happened?"

Cara wiped at a tear trickling down her cheek. "She was diagnosed with cancer shortly after she learned she was pregnant. She couldn't carry the baby and undergo treatment, so she chose to give her baby life instead of saving her own." She sniffed. "That's the kind of unselfish woman she was."

Mason chewed the inside of his cheek. Had the killer known her history?

If he had, would it have made a difference?

Or was he too demented to possess any sense of moral decency at all?

The sheriff approached, his boots crunching the gravel. "Are you finished, Dr. Winchester?"

Cara nodded and dried her eyes. "Yes."

"Cause of death?" the sheriff asked.

"It appears to be exsanguinations, just like Nellie Thompson. He cut out her reproductive organs, as well. But we'll need to verify that with the autopsy."

"So we definitely have a serial killer," Sheriff McRae mumbled. "The press is gonna be all over this."

"We aren't going to reveal the details of the crime," Mason said. "We have to hold back or we'll have copycats trying to take credit for the murders."

"So what do we say?" Sheriff McRae asked.

"I'll talk to one of the profilers from the bureau. She can handle the press and offer a profile to help law enforcement and citizens know who to look for." He showed the flier he'd taken from Sherese to the sheriff and Cara.

"Do you remember this guy, Cara?"

She studied it for a moment, then shook her head. "He could have left it with Sherese when I was gone. You know I divide my time between the BBL, the Winchester Clinic and the res."

"I'm going to question this preacher," Mason said. "Then we'll head to the res. You can talk to Sadie Whitefeather while I meet with Liam Runninghorse about the knife the killer used."

"What about the knife?" Cara asked.

"It's a handmade Native American piece," Mason said. "Since this killer has used the same M.O. twice, he probably used the same type of weapon. If Runninghorse knows someone who favors this knife, maybe it'll lead us to the killer."

HE SAT PERCHED on top of his black stallion, watching as the sheriff and that half-breed Blackpaw combed the grounds near the grave. He'd done his homework on Blackpaw.

The bastard boy had become a tracker for the police.

But he had Indian blood in that brown body of his. And a mean streak that he tried to channel into hunting down those who broke the law.

He was a worthy adversary. A man who would play the game until the end.

Until death came for one of them.

It would be for Blackpaw, but the man didn't know it yet.

He smiled, his blood heating as he'd watched tears fall from Dr. Winchester. She acted like a damn saint.

But she wasn't a saint. She was just as much a whore as the woman in the ground now. Just as much of a sinner.

No, worse. She led the other lambs astray. Taught them to give away their young.

But his people treasured their children more than life itself.

And for her transgressions she had to pay.

A vehicle arrived to transport Yolanda Farraday's body, and he watched the men lift her from the grave. Dirt and debris fluttered down like brown snowflakes, her human remains stiff with rigor and ready to begin the descent into ashes.

He glanced down at his palm and traced a finger over the strands of hair he had removed before he'd put her in the ground. He would thread them into the navel fetish he planned to leave on Dr. Winchester's pillow tonight just as he had threaded Nellie Thompson's hair through the first one.

He wondered if their forensic team had figured out that secret yet.

Still he kept a strand for himself, one that he would weave into the bow that he hung above his bed as a symbol of his devotion to his people and their ways.

One strand for each of the women he would save.

His bow wouldn't be complete until his mission

was complete, and Dr. Winchester lay in the ground beside her lambs where she belonged.

Her hair would be the final strand in his bow, the one to make it complete.

Chapter Eleven

Cara closed her eyes while Mason drove toward Reverend Parch's church. She hated to think that a man who professed to be serving God would use religion as an excuse to murder, but she'd read enough news stories to know that it happened.

"Are you all right, Cara?" Mason asked.

The afternoon sun was starting to fade, gray clouds moving in, adding to the gloomy atmosphere. "Yes."

"Does Yolanda have family?"

"Just an elderly aunt who lives in a nursing home in Corpus Christi. That's the reason she chose the adoption route."

Mason drummed his fingers on the steering wheel. "How about the baby's father?"

"He died in Afghanistan."

"So he's not a suspect." Mason sighed wearily. "Is there anyone associated with one of your patients who lost paternity rights? Or someone who might not have known about their child and only recently found out?"

Cara cut her eyes to him. Obviously that scenario hit too close to home. "At the clinic, our social worker counsels the women regarding their choices. She encourages the women to consult with their baby's father in their decision. And the father has to sign away his rights to make it legal."

His shoulders relaxed slightly. "How about a custody issue? A domestic issue or addiction problem that would have rendered the father unfit to see his child or have a choice in the matter?"

Cara massaged her temple where a headache pulsed. A memory tickled her conscience. A woman named Pauline… "Actually, there was a patient who had to get a restraining order against the man who fathered her baby. He was physically abusive."

Mason perked up. "What was his name?"

"I don't remember, but I can contact our social worker Devon and find out."

"Do it," Mason said as he turned into town and drove down Main Street.

Cara called Devon. After four rings, Devon answered, and Cara quickly explained the situation.

"Pauline's husband is in jail," Devon said. "Has been for six months. He was caught running a meth lab so he won't be out anytime soon."

Cara thanked her and hung up just as Mason pulled into the parking lot.

"What did she say?" Mason asked.

"It's a dead end. Pauline's husband is in prison."

They climbed out, passing a sign that welcomed

all denominations and advertising that the church held two services, one in English and another in Spanish, as they walked to the front of the church.

As they entered, organ music floated through the building. Cara was surprised at the interior. The outside looked faded and worn, but the walls had been painted soft muted colors that reflected the Native American and Mexican influences, and candles flickered on a table with a cross carved in stone above it like a welcoming shrine.

Inside the chapel more candles glowed, adding a somber but calming feel. Stained-glass windows hung above a raised pulpit, allowing light to spill through the crystal colors creating a rainbow effect.

Mason shifted as if uncomfortable. "Let's see if we can find Reverend Parch."

He led the way down the center aisle toward the organ, and a moment later the woman playing it turned toward them.

She was Hispanic with a short, robust build. "Welcome to Our Holy Cross," she said with a beaming smile then grabbed a brochure to give them. "You come about our services?"

"No, we need to talk to Reverend Parch," Mason said. "Is he here?"

"Sí." She gathered her long skirt and gestured for them to follow her. Cara winced as they left the serene sanctity of the chapel and entered a darker hallway that led to the back of the building. It appeared dreary as if they hadn't had time to fix it up yet.

"Dr. Winchester," he said as he stood. "I'm glad you finally decided to accept my invitation and come to church."

Cara shook his hand, a shiver traveling up her back as he squeezed her fingers a little too tightly. His gray eyes skated over her as if he found her unworthy and in need of help.

Mason flashed his credentials, as Cara pulled her hand away. The reverend was much younger than she'd imagined. In fact, he had to be in his early thirties and with his dark hair and arresting eyes, some women probably found him attractive.

But a darkness lurked beneath that calm smile.

"I'm Detective Mason Blackpaw," Mason said. "We have some questions to ask you, Reverend."

Reverend Parch gestured for them to take seats on a dark purple velvet couch in the corner. Cara's legs felt unsteady so she was grateful to sit.

The reverend fiddled with his wire-rimmed glasses then claimed a straight chair across from them, his robe billowing around him.

Cara twisted her hands together. He reminded her of a televangelist who'd charmed followers into donating all their money and worldly goods to join his flock. Just before the police had exposed his scheme, he'd convinced half his congregation to commit mass suicide.

Was she paranoid, or could this reverend actually have committed murder under the guise of saving souls?

MASON DISLIKED Reverend Parch from the moment he laid eyes on him. He had the kind of eyes that told lies with a smile.

He laid the flier Parch had left at the clinic on the coffee table between them. "You brought this by the Winchester Clinic?"

"Yes," the reverend said. "I posted them all over town." He flipped the file on his desk over so Mason couldn't read the name, arousing Mason's curiosity, then leaned forward and crossed his hands on one knee. "I haven't been here long, but my goal is to grow the congregation and to welcome all sorts into our folds."

"All sorts?" Mason asked.

Reverend Parch shrugged. "All nationalities, races, denominations," he said. "We're all God's children. We praise Him together between these walls."

He wondered what else the man did between the walls when doors were closed.

"Did you want to inquire about our services? Or is there something more personal preying on your minds?"

Reverend Parch slanted a pointed look toward Cara, irking Mason more. "Actually, we're here on business. Did you know a young woman named Nellie Thompson?"

The preacher frowned. "Yes, she visited our church. I was so sorry to hear that she died."

"She was murdered," Mason said, deciding to cut

to the chase. He didn't have time to play games. "Would you know anything about that?"

"Just what I read in the paper." Reverend Parch's shoulders stiffened. "I did lead a prayer group for her the night we heard about her death."

Mason studied him. The man was meticulous, calm, cool. Too cool. "Did you know a woman named Yolanda Farraday?"

He stroked the edge of his robe. "No, I can't say that I do."

"She didn't attend your church?" Cara asked.

"Not on a regular basis. But we do have people fill out visitor cards, so she could have stopped in. If so, I haven't had time to contact her personally yet." He went to a basket then sifted though the cards. A moment later, his eyebrows rose. "Yes, as a matter of fact, she visited us last Sunday. Why? Did something happen to her?"

"She was murdered," Mason said. "And we believe she was killed by the same person who killed Nellie Thompson."

Reverend Parch made the sign of the cross. "God bless her soul." Then his eyes narrowed and he frowned. "But I don't understand why you wanted to see me. Are their families worried that they weren't saved before they departed?"

Mason exchanged a look with Cara. "Dr. Winchester received threatening letters aimed toward her clinic, and the killer left a message implying that he believes these women are sinners because they gave their children up for adoption."

A muscle jumped in the reverend's cheek. "I can hardly blame them for expressing their displeasure at what you're doing, Dr. Winchester. You should be trying to keep families together, not tearing them apart."

"I am trying to help them," Cara said tightly.

"Sounds like a personal issue for you." Mason crossed his arms. "You wouldn't happen to be adopted yourself, would you?"

Unease flickered in the preacher's eyes. "As a matter of fact, I was. That's one reason I understand the deep pain a child suffers at the thought of a parent abandoning them."

"Sometimes a mother and or the father choose adoption because they believe it's in the child's best interest."

"How is it in the child's best interest for his mother to throw her child away?"

"You don't know what you're talking about," Cara said stiffly.

"Obviously this topic pushes your buttons, Reverend Parch," Mason cut in. He refused to debate the issue with the man. "We think the killer is using religion to justify his kills."

Realization dawned in the reverend's eyes. "So you want to know if any of my parishioners might fit this description?"

Or if you do.

But Mason held back the accusation.

"Do you?" he asked.

"I'm a man of the cloth, Detective Blackpaw." He turned his gaze toward Cara. "It is my job to help those who are lost. Like you, Doctor, if I break that trust I am no good to those who need me most."

"What kind of answer is that?" Mason asked.

"The only one I can give you."

"Reverend," Cara said. "Two women are dead, and this man may be targeting more. If you know who killed them, you have to tell us before someone else dies."

"Listen to me, Detective, Dr. Winchester. You do your jobs and I'll do mine." He stood. "Now, I think it's time for you to leave."

"Please, Reverend Parch, think about it. If the killer has come to you, convince him to turn himself in," Cara said.

The reverend gave a clipped nod, dismissing them, and they headed to the door. But Mason wasn't sure if he believed the preacher. And if he found anything incriminating the man, he'd be back.

"What did you think?" Cara asked as they settled in his car.

"I don't trust him," Mason said. "Even if he isn't the killer, he may know who is and he's protecting him."

CARA CONTEMPLATED Mason's statement as they drove toward the reservation. The reverend had chosen his words carefully.

Like Mason, she sensed he knew more than he'd said. But no judge would force him to reveal a confession if he'd heard one in confidence.

Could he be the killer? Or if he knew who was, would he convince the man to turn himself in?

The car churned over the ruts in the road as they turned on to the reservation. The sun faded, dipping into the horizon and painting the sky in reds, yellows and orange, the adobe houses blending into the Texas sunset.

"It'll be faster if we split up." Mason drove through the main street and parked at the clinic. "Why don't you talk to Sadie while I visit Runninghorse and inquire about the knife?"

Cara agreed and hopped out, her bulk slowing her down as she made her way into the clinic. She greeted Aponi Bahe, the young woman who volunteered at the clinic, when she entered. "Is Sadie here?" Cara asked.

Aponi nodded and continued cleaning a little boy's scrapes. "In exam room two. She's splinting a hairline fracture."

Cara waved to the little boy, then knocked on the exam room, and Sadie told her to come in.

A little girl with dark eyes looked up from the table where Sadie had splinted her finger. Her mother sat beside her, one hand on the little girl's back for comfort. "There, sweetie," Sadie said, "that should keep it in place so it can heal." Sadie gave the little girl a hug, then helped her down from the table and the mother and child left.

"How are you and baby doing?" Sadie asked.

"We're fine." Cara explained about the murders, the navel fetish she'd received and the note written in blood.

Sadie's face crinkled with worry. "Sit down and let me check you out," she said.

Cara hated being mothered "That's not necessary—"

"Sit, Cara. All this stress can't be good for you and the baby." She coaxed Cara to sit on the exam table then checked her blood pressure.

"Normal, isn't it?"

"Actually it's a little high," Sadie said with a frown. "You need to take it easy, Cara."

"I can't," Cara said. "Not until we find out who killed two of my patients." She forced herself to take slow, even breaths while Sadie listened to her heart, then the baby's.

"Mason thinks the killer is targeting my patients because of my work at the women's clinic."

Sadie's eyes widened. "Then he thinks you're in danger?"

Cara shrugged off her concern. "I gave Mason the hate mail I received," Cara said. "But because of the amulet the killer left me, he thinks the killer has Native American roots."

Sadie leaned against the sink. "You think the killer might be from the res?"

Cara hated to disparage any of the Native American people. They already faced enough prejudices. "I don't know, but it's possible. He buried the women in a Comanche ritualistic style."

Sadie's eyes flickered with unease.

"So either he has Indian roots or has studied the culture. The crimes also have religious undertones and my clinic, specifically adoptions, seem to have triggered his violence." She stood and paced, thinking. "Is there anyone you know of on the res who fits this description? Anyone who may have a grudge against me?"

Sadie thumped her finger on her chin. "The only person I can think of is Isabella Morningside's ex-husband."

"Isabella?" Cara said, the name tickling her memory banks. "She did say her husband changed when he came home from overseas. He was angry, violent. I urged her to get him into counseling."

"He refused and his behavior became so erratic, she divorced him," Sadie said. "He lost all rights to his unborn baby and blames you. At least that's what Isabella said."

Was he killing her patients and cutting out their reproductive organs because he really wanted to do that to his ex-wife?

HE LET HIMSELF INSIDE Dr. Winchester's cabin, eager to leave her his gift.

The scent of some kind of lavender bath wash

swirled around him as he walked through the small den. The Native American decor in the room soothed him, but it was lost on Cara Winchester.

She was not a Native. She had no ties to his people.

Except for the baby she carried.

Anger churned through him, heating his blood, and he made his way to her bedroom. The sight of her flannel gown at the foot of the bed belied the fact that she had seduced Blackpaw into getting her pregnant.

And that she'd planned to leave him out of his child's life just as she encouraged other women to do.

The bitch had no moral code.

But he did. He honored the sanctity of the family unit.

Hatred for the doctor emboldened him and he smeared blood on her gown, then laid the navel fetish on her pillow. His pulse pounding with adrenaline, he carefully placed the note he'd written with Yolanda's blood beside it.

Sweet pleasure stole through him as he imagined the doctor's face when she found it.

Time for him to hunt another now.

He had too much work to do to linger....

Chapter Twelve

Mason always felt at home on the reservation. After all, he'd grown up on this land, and knew every inch of it by heart. He treasured the culture of his people, and it pained him to suspect one of his own as the ruthless killer who'd robbed two women of their lives.

But crime knew no boundaries or lines. And if it was one of his own, he'd do whatever necessary to bring him in.

Runninghorse was working on sharpening a set of knives when he approached. Liam served on the Tribal Council, but he'd also built a business selling Native American weapons. Local tourist shops as well as stores in San Antonio, El Paso, and Corpus Christi carried his wares. They'd been friends since they were boys.

He shook Mason's hand. "Nice to see you, man."

"I wish it was a social visit," Mason said. "But I'm afraid it's about a case I'm working on."

Liam gestured for Mason to step outside with

him. Mason breathed in the fresh air, the sound of wildlife rustling through the neighboring woods a reminder of his early childhood days when Liam's father had taught both of them to hunt and fish.

"It's about the woman who was murdered?" Liam asked.

Mason nodded. "There are two victims now." He explained what they'd uncovered so far. "Do you have a repeat customer who bought this particular knife?"

"I sell a lot of those," Liam said. "Most collectors want a variety though instead of multiple versions of the same weapon."

"Anyone on the res favor the buffalo skinner?"

Liam's jaw hardened. "Half the men on the res have one, and so do the adolescent boys. I can give you the names of the stores I serve, too. Maybe they can check their orders and see if anything jumps out."

Probably a dead end.

He had another thought. "Has there been trouble on the res lately? Anyone the tribal police had to deal with?"

Liam quirked his head in thought. "Actually Lapu Morningside. When he returned from the service, he wasn't the same. Think he suffered a head trauma. Has PTSD. Whatever the cause, the police were called to his house several times before his wife divorced him."

The hair on the back of Mason's neck bristled. At

the second crime scene, he'd found that button that looked as if it came from a military uniform. "Does he have children?"

Liam nodded. "Wife had a baby last year while he was deployed. But she took out a restraining order against him and cut him off from seeing the child."

Mason frowned. Not exactly the background scenario he'd expected of the killer, but Morningside apparently had issues. Maybe he was venting his rage against his wife on other women?

"Does he live on the res now?"

"No." Liam stuffed his hands in the pockets of his suede jacket. "Tribal police forced him to leave. I don't know where he is."

So the man had served his country, was suffering PTSD, had been cut off from his child and the reservation?

All those circumstances could have triggered him to snap and start killing.

His cell phone buzzed, and he thanked Running-horse, then headed to his car to meet Cara. He connected the call as he slid behind the steering wheel. "Blackpaw."

"Detective Blackpaw, this is Special Agent Julie Whitehead of the FBI."

Mason frowned. He'd been expecting this call. "Go on."

"I spoke with Sheriff McRae about your serial killer."

"Yes."

"I'll be in town in an hour, and I'd like to meet with you and comprise a profile. The press is hungry for information. It would be better if we issue a statement before they print something that's going to blow your case or create panic."

She had a point. "All right, I'll meet you at the sheriff's office in a couple of hours."

"Do you have any leads?"

Mason clenched the steering wheel as he parked at the res clinic. "Nothing concrete. But you can have your people do background checks on Reverend Webber Parch and another man named Lapu Morningside. I'll explain my suspicions when we meet."

"I'll get right on it," Agent Whitehead said.

Mason thanked her, then disconnected the call and climbed from the car just as Cara stepped outside.

Suddenly the air around him stirred, and Mason's gut instincts spiked, warning him something was wrong.

A heartbeat later, a bullet whizzed by his head, racing toward Cara.

THE HISS OF A GUNSHOT skimmed by Cara's face, startling her.

Suddenly Mason shouted her name and threw himself at her. Another shot rang out, the air hot with fear as she clawed at Mason to remain upright.

Mason yanked her into the doorway and shoved her behind him. "Dammit, Cara, stay down."

Two kids playing nearby screamed and ducked inside the diner next door. A pickup truck rolled past, another car's muffler rumbled from somewhere in the distance. Three teenagers smoking across the way must have heard it because they hightailed it to a beat-up Chevy.

Panic robbed Cara's breath as Mason wielded his gun, then used the edge of the door for cover and searched for the shooter.

Dear God, someone *had* tried to kill her.

Protective instincts for her unborn child kicked in, and anger surged through her.

Mason looked left then right and muttered a curse. "I don't see him."

She scanned the street, but she didn't see anything out of place, either. "Maybe he was on a rooftop."

Mason nodded and glanced up, his gaze moving from one rooftop to another.

"I called the tribal police," Sadie said from behind her.

"Stay back," Mason warned.

A second later, a siren wailed, and the chief's car swerved up in front of the clinic. Bradford Pann, the chief of the tribal police, emerged from the SUV, his gun poised, Liam Runninghorse with him.

"Someone shot at Dr. Winchester," Mason said as he inched from behind the doorway.

Chief Pann conducted a visual sweep, then strode toward them. "You all right, Dr. Winchester?"

"Yes, thanks to Detective Blackpaw."

Mason must have seen the blood on her face because his eyes blazed with rage. "He did hit you."

"It's just a flesh burn," Cara said shrugging it off.

"Did you see the shooter?" Chief Pann asked.

"No," Cara said.

Mason growled in his throat. "Me neither. I pulled up and saw Cara coming out then heard the shot." He gestured to Cara. "Go inside with Sadie while we search the streets. For all we know, he's still out here waiting to take another shot."

Cara wanted to help, but he was right. She couldn't take chances when she was nine months pregnant.

Her gaze met Mason's. "Just be careful."

Anger hardened his expression but underneath it, other emotions simmered. Mason was a lawman, a protector.

And he was the father of her baby.

Even if he didn't love her, he would protect her and their child with his life.

MASON BARELY CONTROLLED his rage. If anything had happened to Cara and his son, he didn't know what he would do.

But he would damn well find the bastard who'd shot at her and make him pay.

"Do you have any idea which direction the shot came from?" Chief Pann asked.

Mason struggled to calm himself. Cara was safe inside with Sadie. The best thing he could do was focus on his job.

He forced himself to analyze the situation from a lawman's perspective and tried to recreate the shooting in his mind. He had been parked, about to get out when he'd heard the gunshot. He closed his eyes, mentally summoning the details. The sound of the gunshot cracking the air, the speed of its movement, the angle it had come from. To his right…

He pivoted, mentally judging the angle and trajectory and studied the buildings. "I think it came from somewhere over there."

Chief Pann scowled. "The feed store?"

Mason nodded, and Liam gave him an understanding look. "Probably from the roof." Mason and Liam went to check it out while the chief searched the clinic front for bullet casings.

The feed store was deserted and in need of repairs. Mason strode up the back stairs to the roof, climbed on top and began to scavenge the area.

The rotting boards of the ceiling squeaked as he crossed to the spot where he thought the shooter had probably been standing. He gauged the distance and studied where Cara had been.

"There are footprints here," Liam said.

"We'll take a cast of the prints." Mason knelt and examined the print, then noted something sticky and yellow on the floorboard. Maybe resin of some kind.

He'd take a sample of that for analysis.

"Here are the shell casings," Liam said.

Mason used a handkerchief to pick them up. He'd have them tested, as well.

"Someone didn't like you asking questions on the res," Liam commented.

"Obviously," Mason muttered.

Was it the same man who'd killed Nellie Thompson and Yolanda Farraday?

Probably.

But the killer had preferred the buffalo skinner as his weapon in the murders. So why shoot at Cara?

Because they were getting too close to the truth, too close to finding him?

Or did Cara have more than one enemy?

"Did you find out anything from Sadie?" Mason asked.

Cara explained about Morningside.

"Runninghorse mentioned him, too," Mason said. "Sounds as though he has a grudge." And if he did, Mason would find him and put him in jail.

AN HOUR LATER, Cara and Mason drove back to town. But Cara kept reliving the shooting, her terror for her baby making her edgy.

"You should go into protective custody until this case is solved," Mason said as he wound toward the sheriff's office. "I'm meeting an FBI agent now and we'll arrange a safe house."

Cara tensed. Part of her wanted to run and hide

and take care of herself. But her patients depended on her. "Mason, I can't do that. If I run, he wins."

Mason parked the car and turned to her, a gruffness in his eyes that made her throat close. "This is not a game, Cara. Your life—our son's life—is in danger."

"I realize that," Cara said, barely resisting a shiver. "But I also know that you'll protect us."

Mason's eyes darkened with fear. "I will. But what if it's not enough?"

Cara's heart melted. As tough and strong as this cowboy cop was, he had a heart of gold and a soft spot for women and kids.

Still, it didn't mean he wanted to marry her or that he loved her.

Just that he felt responsible, and he lived to do his job. To protect people from maniacs like the one who'd killed two of her patients.

A shudder coursed through her. For all she knew, the killer was stalking his next victim now.

She reached out and laid her hand over Mason's. "I trust you, Mason. But I've done nothing wrong and neither have these women. If this man wants me, then I have to show him he can't stop me from doing my job. Or from helping my patients."

"Cara—"

"Shh." She pressed a finger to his lips, desperately wanting to press her mouth there. "I told you, I trust you to protect me and our baby. Now let's find this guy before he kills again."

That statement took the fight from him.

"Come on, I want to hear what this agent has to say." Cara reached for the door handle but Mason caught her hand.

"Cara, promise me you'll stay with me. That you won't go off on your own and do something to piss this guy off even more."

"I promise." Cara offered him an encouraging smile although she hadn't meant to tick the killer off in the first place. And if he was as irrational as they believed, he was delusional, living in his own world, inventing his own reasons to justify his actions, and it had nothing to do with her.

MASON HAD TO REIGN in his caveman instincts or else he'd hog-tie Cara and lock her up in a room himself.

God help him. No one would hurt her or his son. He'd die first.

They entered the sheriff's office together, and McRae showed them to a small conference room off his office. He made the introductions and Julie Whitehead, a blonde, blue-eyed woman who looked as if she should be a model instead of special agent, shook their hands.

"Thanks for coming, Detective Blackpaw, Dr. Winchester."

They seated themselves around a table where she'd laid out photographs of both crime scenes, the history of the victims, information on the Winchester Clinic as well as the suspects they'd interviewed.

"I see you've done your homework," Mason said.

Special Agent Whitehead nodded. "I want to get this profile out to the press and other law enforcement agencies ASAP."

"It's time to warn the women, don't you think?" Cara asked.

"We'll issue a general warning," Agent Whitehead said. "But we only have two victims so far, so it's too soon to say for certain that all the victims are patients of yours. Also, technically we need three victims to call this a serial killer."

"I feel responsible," Cara said.

"It's not your fault," Agent Whitehead said. "Timing, the suspect's mental condition, some circumstance or trigger that we don't even know about yet—they're all factors beyond your control."

"Are you ready to talk to the press?" Mason asked.

She nodded. "I've prepared the profile, and Sheriff McRae has agreed to stand with me." She gestured toward a file. "I've also compiled the information on the two men you asked me to check into, Detective."

"And?"

"Reverend Parch looks good on paper. Too good. But we're still digging into his background."

"And Morningside?"

"I have an address. You were right. Morningside sustained serious injuries in Afghanistan and received a medical discharge. He's supposed to be on medication to treat his psychological condition, but he doesn't like taking meds, so he's a loose cannon."

He also had a grudge against Cara, had lived on the res, had easy access to a buffalo skinner, and could have known he and Cara were at the res today and taken that shot.

Mason heaved a breath. "I'll check out his place tonight."

Agent Whitehead nodded. "Let me do the press conference and I'll go with you."

He brought Cara some tea and himself some coffee while the sheriff greeted reporters from the local paper, the local TV stations and lawmen from adjoining counties. Two reporters from news stations in Houston and El Paso also showed up.

Special Agent Whitehead looked poised and confident in her dark suit as she stepped in front of the cameras.

Sheriff McRae relayed the fact that they had had two murders targeted to women, specifically single mothers, but held back details regarding the navel fetish and blood notes the killer had left behind. Then he introduced Agent Whitehead.

"We now believe we're dealing with a serial offender," she said. "Police, law enforcement agencies and citizens should be vigilant. We believe the killer is a male in his twenties, possibly Native American or mixed heritage. Judging from his M.O., he has strong ties to the Native American culture and most likely suffered some kind of traumatic loss recently. Since he appears to be targeting single mothers, more specifically in the case of our two victims, women who have offered their children for adoption, we believe the adoption angle is his trigger, that he was most likely abandoned as a child. Quite possibly, he grew up in an orphanage or foster home, but he could have been adopted yet never fit into that family. He is educated but due to his social inadequacies, may not be able to hold a job or feels demeaned by his current one." She paused. "He also may have obsessive compulsive tendencies with cleanliness and may be suffering from delusions that he is serving God by committing these crimes. If you know of anyone who fits the profile, please call your local police or the FBI."

As soon as she finished her speech, hands flew up, questions coming.

"So what is this guy's M.O.?"

"I'm not at liberty to reveal specific details of the crimes at this point for fear of interfering with the investigation," Agent Whitehead said.

"Was the break-in at the Winchester Clinic related to the murders?" another reporter asked.

Agent Whitehead remained calm. "We can't confirm that at this time."

"Do you have any suspects?" another one asked.

Agent Whitehead continued to dodge questions for the next few minutes, and Mason grew antsy.

Finally Agent Whitehead turned the microphone over to Sheriff McRae. "As Agent Whitehead asked, please contact the police if you have any information regarding this case."

McRae answered more questions while Mason herded Cara through the back door, ushering the agent to join them so they could sneak out the back.

Cara remained quiet as they drove toward Morningside's apartment, a hole-in-the-wall on the outside of town that had seen better days. Scrub brush and dried grass dotted the forgotten property, the sagging buildings attesting to the age and the low-income renters that lived there.

"If Morningside is our man," Special Agent Whitehead said, "we need to tread carefully, Detective Blackpaw. With PTSD sufferers, he may be so delusional he won't even know who we are."

Mason bit back a curse. She might feel sorry for the guy because of his condition, but if he had butchered two woman and tried to hurt Cara, no excuse was going to get him off.

THAT DAMN BLACKPAW had called in a stupid agent. Dumb bitch.

She thought he was socially inadequate.

Fool. She had no idea what she was talking about. Or what he was capable of.

He shut off the TV with a curse, then checked his list.

Angelica Mansfield. Her friends called her Angel.

But she was no angel. The devil had gotten into her soul.

He traced a finger over the edges of the bow on his wall, pleased with the strands of hair that he'd woven into it. It wasn't finished yet, far from it.

Angel's long red strands would go next.

Chapter Thirteen

Cara followed Mason and the special agent up the sidewalk to Morningside's apartment door. A few beat-up cars were scattered across the parking lot, the building weathered and dark. The lights that should have illuminated the sidewalks were burned out, the deserted buildings a place for criminals and those who didn't want to be found to hide out.

"Stay behind me and Agent Whitehead, Cara," Mason said. "And if there's any sign of trouble run to the car."

Cara clenched her hands into fists. She hated to be treated like the weakling, but she was smart enough to know that he was right. He and the FBI agent were armed.

She was pregnant and the focus of this man's rage.

They made their way to the corner unit, bugs buzzing around the doorway. Mason knocked and they waited, but no one answered. Mason pressed his ear to the door to listen for someone inside, then shook his head.

"I don't hear anyone."

Agent Whitehead arched a brow, her hand on her gun as she faked a smile. "I don't know, I think I heard something. Maybe someone's in trouble in there."

Cara understood her underlying meaning. They had to have probable cause to enter, and they had none. Unless they invented a reason, and they all seemed fine with that.

Mason used a lockpicking tool to open the door then gently nudged her into the corner of the foyer. "Stay here while we clear the place."

She nodded, her lungs squeezing for air as she waited for them to search the apartment.

What if Morningside was hiding upstairs? What if he ambushed Mason and hurt him?

MASON RUSHED THROUGH the second floor of the apartment to clear it. There was only one bedroom and bath, both dingy and dark rooms with minimalistic furnishings. A chair, ratty dresser, an unmade bed.

Agent Whitehead stepped into the bathroom to examine the contents while he checked the closet. He found a couple pairs of jeans and a few T-shirts, a pair of military issued boots, fatigues, an army duffel bag and a dress uniform.

A button was missing on the sleeve.

A button that looked like the one he'd found at the landfill.

He'd have to bag it for analysis though to be sure.

"Looks like he's been staying here," Agent White-head said. "Toothbrush was still damp."

"Confiscate it for DNA," Mason said. "I'm going to take this uniform in to compare it to the button we found at the second crime scene."

Downstairs he thought he heard footsteps, then a scream, and remembered Cara. Dammit. Had Morningside returned?

His heart pounding, he raced down the steps. The front door was wide open and Cara was sprawled on the floor.

"He came to the door and saw me," Cara gasped. "Then he shoved me and ran. Go after him, Mason!"

Agent Whitehead followed on his heels. "Stay with Cara," he shouted.

He jogged outside, searching the property. He didn't see movement in the parking lot, so he inched around the bushes to the right. Darkness shrouded the exterior, the wooded area nearby thick with trees and brush.

Braced for an ambush, he crept around the side of the building, keeping close to the edge, his eyes scanning the area. A car engine rumbled in the distance, sputtering as it careened away from the complex.

Was he wrong? Had Morningside headed to the parking lot to make his escape?

Or was he in the woods?

He detected movement a few feet away, a bush

rustling. A tree branch cracked then leaves fluttered down. He jogged toward the woods, eyes peeled, ears in tune to the sounds of nature to weed out the animals from the sound of footsteps.

Or a man breathing.

Forcing himself to stay focused, he crept between the mesquites, then chased the shadow. He raced over a tree stump and group of logs, speeding up as he darted past a clump of brush. Another engine fired up, and just as he made it through the clearing, an SUV peeled down the road.

Dammit, he'd lost him.

Frustrated, he strode back through the woods, anxious to see Cara. By the time he reached the apartment, he was cursing himself.

He stomped up to the door and stepped inside. "Cara? Agent Whitehead?"

The agent met him at the door. "She's fine," the agent said as if she sensed his concern. "But you have to see this."

Mason followed her through the entryway to a den, then into a small alcove.

Cara stood at the edge of the space, her face pale.

He pressed a hand to her back. "Are you okay, Cara?"

"Yes." But when she angled her head toward him, she didn't look okay at all.

Then he saw what had upset her.

On the wall above the metal desk a bulletin board was filled with photographs of her. Pictures of her as she left the clinic in town, other shots of her on the reservation walking a patient outside, then photos of her cabin on BBL property.

Other disturbing items covered the board, as well. Articles on the opening of the women's pavilion, other news clippings about conspiracy theories, about the downfall of society and the family unit, Bible verses written on note cards, and other printouts of Native American customs and beliefs.

There were also news clippings of the Thompson and Farraday murders.

"It's him, isn't it?" Cara asked in a strained voice.

Mason swallowed hard. "Judging from this, it looks that way."

He knotted his hands into fists. And he had just let the sick bastard escape.

A CHILL ENGULFED Cara as she studied the articles and photos on Morningside's wall. He definitely seemed to fit the profile Agent Whitehead had described.

He was obsessed with conspiracy theories, Native American beliefs, and with her.

Knowing he had watched her from a distance, had photographed her and kept tabs on her whereabouts, made her feel violated all over.

Agent Whitehead retrieved her phone from her belt. "I'll call Sheriff McRae and have him send someone out here ASAP."

"Tell him to issue an APB on Morningside, as well. This guy is dangerous and has to be stopped."

"I'll call my office and see what else they can find out about Morningside's background. His military career could tell us a lot."

She stepped outside the apartment on the stoop to make the call, and Mason turned to her. "Cara, are you all right?"

She lifted her gaze to his. "I can't believe he's so fixated on me. All I did was try to counsel his wife. But he blames me for their break-up."

"You did what you had to do for her," Mason said. "This man obviously has psychological problems, so encouraging her to leave him was the right thing to do."

Cara frowned. "But why would he take out his rage on those other women?"

Mason contemplated the question. "His thinking is skewed. Now he's venting his anger against them, but he may eventually go after the real source, his wife."

"I have to warn her," Cara said.

"Yes, call her," Mason said. "I'll phone Running-horse and alert the tribal police."

Cara nodded, grateful to be given a task. She needed to focus, to do something to help stop Morningside, not just dwell on her guilt and fear. She slipped back to the living area, seated herself in a corner chair and punched in Isabella's number.

When she didn't answer, Cara left a message then phoned Sadie.

"You think Morningside is the serial killer?" Sadie asked.

Cara hesitated. She hated to accuse him of such a serious crime, but judging from the wall and the fact that he'd run, it was possible. "I don't know, but he's definitely dangerous." Cara explained about their findings. "Just be careful, Sadie."

"Don't worry, Carter hasn't left me alone a second since the first murder occurred," Sadie said with a laugh.

Cara smiled. She was so glad to see Sadie happy and in love. Carter, who had been falsely imprisoned for five years, deserved happiness, as well.

Still, she was nervous as she hung up. What if Morningside was so panicked that he went after his ex-wife now?

She found Mason photographing the disturbing wall and relayed her concerns.

"Runninghorse is going to guard Isabella's place tonight. We'll put her under protective custody until her ex is caught."

The crime unit arrived moments later, and Mason put them to work scouring the man's apartment.

"Look for specific evidence regarding the two women he murdered so far," Mason said. He showed them the uniform he'd found and asked them to log it into evidence.

Cara remembered the button they'd found at the

dump site and realized Mason thought it was probably a match.

"What about the murder weapon?" she asked.

Mason shook his head. "I searched while you were on the phone and didn't find it."

Cara shivered. That could mean that the man had it with him and that he was hunting down another victim now.

Mason searched Morningside's browser history on his computer. Articles similar to the ones posted on the bulletin board had been reviewed, and he had definitely Googled Cara.

Anger tasted bitter on his tongue. The man had found out everything he could about Cara, including her family history, where she'd attended school, photos of the honors she'd received in medical school, where she lived.

He searched further, hunting through files to see if he had a list of Cara's clients and was using them as targets. But he didn't find a list.

Of course, that didn't mean the man didn't have it on him.

He checked Morningside's phone, then called the lab that was processing the evidence collected in all the cases and asked to speak to Jody. "Nellie Thompson received a message before she died. See if that call came from this number."

He gave her the number and waited while she checked. When she returned a moment later, she sighed. "I'm afraid not. The message came from a throwaway burner phone. There's no way we can track it down."

"How about that button from the uniform? Did you find prints on it?"

"Yes, a partial. I'm running it now."

"Look for a man named Lapu Morningside. He was in the military so his prints should be in the system."

"Hang on," Jody said. "This might take a minute."

"I'll wait." Mason paced back to the living room where Cara was waiting. She looked exhausted and shaken.

And so damn beautiful he wanted to wrap her in his arms and promise her that everything would be all right.

"Detective Blackpaw," Jody said, cutting into his thoughts. "You were right. It's a match."

Mason sucked in a sharp breath. That print confirmed that Morningside was at the landfill where the second body had been found. "Thanks, Jody. We might just have enough to nail this creep."

He disconnected, then went to tell Agent Whitehead and the other crime analysts. "I just confirmed that the button we discovered at the second crime scene came from Morningside's uniform. Take his computer and anything else you find." He remembered Cara's haunted look. "I'm going to drive Cara home. Let me know if you turn up anything signifi-

cant. When we catch Morningside, we have to make
sure he stays in jail."

Agent Whitehead agreed to supervise the search
and to follow up with the sheriff.

"Now he knows we're on to him, he may try to
run," Mason said.

"I'll alert authorities, bus and train stations, the
airport and the border patrol in case he tries to flee
into Mexico."

Satisfied he'd done all he could at the moment,
he went to Cara. Relief softened her face when he
explained about the call from the lab and their plan
of action.

"I hope they find him tonight, so this terrible ordeal can end," Cara said as he walked her to the car.

So did he. And he wouldn't rest until this madman
was found, and Cara and his son were out of danger.

TENSION STRETCHED BETWEEN Cara and Mason as they
left the apartment. Cara was exhausted and simply
wanted to go home and sleep, but Mason insisted
they stop for dinner, that she needed to feed their
child. She couldn't argue with that.

She made it through a dish of chicken potpie
while he wolfed down a couple of burgers at the
local diner, then they settled in for the ride to the
BBL.

She must have dozed off as soon as they left the
diner, because one minute she'd fastened her seat
belt, and the next Mason was parking at her cabin.

He opened her car door for her while she struggled with the seat belt. The baby kicked just as she tried to stand, and pain shot down her leg. She gripped the door edge and breathed through it. Although she had reached that uncomfortable nine-month stage, she wasn't ready for labor, at least not tonight.

Her emotions were too raw from the day's stress.

"Cara?" Mason said gruffly.

"I'm fine," she said, straightening. "Just a Braxton Hicks contraction."

"Are you sure?"

"Yes." She couldn't quite meet his eyes. She wasn't ready to deal with his part in her son's life, either.

Not that he would want to be there on a daily basis. Even when they'd made love months ago, he'd never said he loved her.

No, the only thing Mason Blackpaw loved was his job.

And it took him all over the state so if he wanted to be a part of their baby's life, it would be on his terms. He'd be a drop-in father.

And she would have to live with it.

She waddled toward the front door, wincing as her back throbbed, then climbed the steps, grateful to be home. Mason opened the door, and she stepped inside,

"I'm going to lie down," she said, oblivious to anything but resting her head on her pillow and forgetting about the day.

"Go ahead. I'll find Brody and fill him in. I want to email a photograph of Morningside to the staff and security guards to warn them to be on watch."

The reminder of the man who'd fixated his rage on her and the women he'd murdered made her shudder with revulsion. But she forced herself not to look at Mason or else she'd fall into his arms and beg him to hold her.

She heard him talking on the phone as she walked into her bedroom. She flipped on the light, then reached for her gown, but the moment she glanced at the bed, bile rose to her throat.

Her gown had bloody streaks across it.

And another note written in blood and a small box were nestled beside it.

Dear God, the killer had been here again. And that blood probably belonged to Yolanda Farraday.

HE WOUND THE STRANDS of Angelica's long red hair around his fingers, soaking in the silky texture and color.

Her scream had pierced the air so loudly that it had hurt his ears.

But no one had heard. He'd made sure of that. A laugh bubbled in his throat.

She lay stiff, her pale body streaked with blood, her lips parted in a soundless scream, her eyes wide with the horror of death.

She had fought the hardest.

So hard she had dug her nails into his skin.

He couldn't have that.

He removed the manicure scissors from his pocket and clipped her nails so close to the skin that blood trickled off her fingertips. He hated the mess, but he couldn't leave evidence behind.

Another reason he had shaved his body. Not that he had much hair. None on his chest thanks to his Native American heritage.

He dropped her nail clippings into a baggie and stuffed them in his pocket, then rolled her in the sheet. Now he had to find the perfect place to leave her.

Some place where that Indian cop and Dr. Winchester would see her.

Some place where that stupid FBI agent would recognize that he was smarter than she was.

And that he was far from finished.

Chapter Fourteen

Cara's gasp brought Mason racing to the bedroom. He saw the bloody note and gown and pulled Cara away from the sight. "Son of a bitch."

Cara choked back a cry, and he wrapped his arms around her and rocked her in his arms. "Shh, it's okay. That creep just wants to taunt you. Don't let him get to you."

"How can I not?" Cara whispered. "He's killing these women because of me."

He forced her to look into his eyes. "No, he's killing them because he's sick. He's only using you as an excuse, and we're not going to let him win."

"But that's probably Yolanda's blood," she said, her voice breaking.

Unless he had killed again and they hadn't found the body yet.

But Mason refused to scare her with that horrid thought. Instead, he had to soothe her. She was a dedicated doctor who'd devoted her life to saving lives and helping others.

She didn't deserve this kind of torture.

"Come on, Cara, step back into the living room while I take care of this."

She shook her head, then inhaled sharply and gathered her strength. "I have to see what's inside that box."

He hesitated but decided it was futile to argue. But he did retrieve gloves and put them on before he handled anything. He bagged the gown and note, then opened the box.

Just as before, it held a navel fetish.

Cara's breathing rattled out in the tension-laden air, then she leaned closer to take a better look at the amulet.

"My God, Mason," she whispered. "That looks like human hair woven around the pouch."

Mason's breath caught as he examined it. Dammit, she was right.

The killer had not only used his victim's blood to write the note, but he'd woven her hair into the navel amulet.

"I'll have the lab verify it and examine the first amulet to see if he included a strand of Nellie Thompson's hair with it."

"That is so twisted," Cara said. "I can't imagine how his mind works."

Mason lifted his eyes to hers. "Most serial killers keep a trophy from their victim, Cara. My guess is that he's keeping a strand of the women's hair as his souvenir."

THE THOUGHT OF MORNINGSIDE, or any other man, being so cruel and ruthless made Cara feel ill.

"I have to take a shower," she said. She had to clean off the stench of what this man had done. She grabbed a clean nightgown and rushed into the bathroom, desperate to escape the images bombarding her.

Poor Nellie and Yolanda, helpless, trapped by a madman who'd butchered them. Then he cut strands of their hair to keep as a trophy.

Tears blurred her eyes as she stripped and climbed beneath the warm spray of water. She glanced down at her big belly and forced herself to remember that she was physically safe for now.

That her son was alive and healthy, growing inside her, and that Mason would protect them. But the memory of that earlier nightmare taunted her.

She wouldn't allow this man to take her son away. She'd protect him with her life.

Still, her emotions were so raw she didn't bother fighting the tears. She let them fall. Tears of grief for the two women who'd lost their lives. Tears for the futures he'd stolen.

Tears of fear that he might be out there hurting someone else now.

The idea that he might be stalking another one of her patients terrified her. She needed to warn them to leave town until this madman was caught.

Breathing steadier now she had a plan of action, she scrubbed her skin and hair, then let the warm water massage away the tension in her body. It must have worked because the baby began to kick vigorously, reminding her he was alive and would be born soon.

She couldn't wait to hold him in her arms.

What would he look like?

She instantly imagined Mason's striking dark hair and big brown eyes. His high cheekbones and the rugged set of his jaw.

He would be a heartbreaker if he looked like his father.

And a reminder to her every day that she loved the man who'd given her a son.

Even if he walked away from them when the investigation was over.

MASON ALERTED BRODY and the security guards on the BBL and emailed Morningside's photo to the staff. While Cara showered, he had to distract himself so he stripped her bed and changed her sheets, then phoned the lab.

"Jody, I hate to bother you again tonight, but our guy left another navel fetish and bloody note at Dr. Winchester's. He took it a step further and also smeared blood on one of her gowns."

"He's making it personal," she said, her voice tinged with disgust.

She was right. The blood on Cara's gown indicated he would come after her soon. "There's something else. There's a strand of hair woven into the pouch. I think it's human hair, probably belongs to the victim. Check the first one and see if there's a strand of hair there, then compare it to Nellie Thompson's."

"I was going to call you about that," Jody said. "I noticed it earlier and ran some tests. You're right, it was the victim's."

Mason ground his jaw. "He's probably keeping a strand for himself." He hadn't found the hair at Morningside's, but he could have hidden it. "Jody, look at the evidence collected from Morningside's apartment. See if the crime techs found anything with hair in it. He wove it through these amulets. He could have woven it into something else."

"I'll get on it ASAP," Jody said. "But it would really help if we could find that knife."

Hell, he knew that.

It was another loose end that worried him.

But Morningside probably had it with him.

Although another thought struck him. This guy was so sick he might be keeping his souvenir with him, either in some kind of container or pouch, or he could have woven the hair into something he was wearing.

Something like a hat or earring or belt, something he could wear in public and flaunt his secret without giving himself away.

The door opened, and Cara appeared, her long hair damp from the shower, her face scrubbed clean.

But her eyes were red-rimmed and puffy, and he instantly knew she'd been crying.

"Cara?" His voice cracked with the effort it took not to drag her into his arms.

"Please tell me we'll stop him."

Her whispered plea tore him to pieces.

"I won't let him hurt you or our baby," he said, his heart in his eyes.

Her lower lip quivered, and his resolve to remain professional flew out the door. He pulled her into his arms and held her tight.

Cara leaned into him, clutching him as if she was afraid to let go.

For once he didn't want her to. Maybe he never had.

Unable to stop himself, he tilted her chin up with his thumb and closed his mouth over hers.

CARA FELT RAW AND EXPOSED, but she needed Mason, and she was too weak and tired to resist. His mouth touched hers, enflaming her with emotions and desire and the love she'd tried so hard to deny.

It swelled inside her though, aching and empty, a hole that needed to be filled.

His hands caressed her face as he deepened the kiss, one digging into her hair and the other skating down to her waist as he pulled her closer to him. Her belly bulged between them, a reminder she was about as sexy as a cow, but he didn't seem to notice.

Instead, he growled low in his throat and deepened the kiss by delving his tongue inside her mouth.

She parted her lips on a breathy sigh and eagerly welcomed the mating dance as she suckled his tongue and traced one finger down his jaw. The rough, unshaven texture sent a thrill through her, just as his hand did when he cupped her bottom and backed her toward the bed.

He pulled off her robe, and Cara blushed as his gaze fell on the flannel maternity gown. "I'm huge," she whispered, then started to pull away.

His eyes darkened with passion and stirred her lust. Then he gently eased her down on the bed.

She felt clumsy and awkward as he stretched out beside her. But his hand fell across her abdomen and a wonderful sweetness flickered in his eyes, followed by the protective, masculine gleam that had stolen her heart the first time she'd met him.

"Mason—"

"Shh," he murmured. "Let me hold you and take care of you all night."

Emotions nearly choked her, and she nodded, too moved to trust herself to speak. Then he shucked his clothes down to his boxers, and gestured to her gown.

"Please," he said on a sigh.

"Mason, you may not like what you see now."

A sliver of anger flashed briefly on his face. "Trust me, Cara. I just want us to be close. I won't push you for anything more."

Except God help her, she wanted more. She wanted all of him.

She wanted his hands all over her, touching her, kissing her.

Making love to her.

But the baby kicked and another contraction seized her stomach, and she had to settle for what he offered.

He hadn't said forever or that he loved her.

Just that he wanted to hold her tonight.

She would ask nothing more.

Then the pain wouldn't be so intense when he left.

He reached for the buttons on her gown, and she blushed again, then allowed him to peel the fabric away. Still, she was vastly out of shape, so she closed her eyes, unable to bear his reaction the first time he saw her pregnant form.

Her breasts were heavy and achy, her belly button had popped out, and in spite of all those creams that everyone spouted prevented stretch marks, the faint line of one darkened her middle.

"Cara." His whispered word brushed her ear, then his kiss followed, a stream of them trailing down her neck to her breasts. Her eyes flew open, and she swallowed hard, her breathing erratic as he tilted her face toward his.

"You are beautiful." He laid one hand on her abdomen, and her throat thickened with the words that she had to hold back.

Then he kissed her tenderly, dragged her into his

arms and cradled her against his bare chest. Her heart pounded with the tenderness in his embrace, yet her blood sizzled from the need to make love to him.

But he didn't push or ask. Instead, he treated her with reverence, as if she was a precious gift in his arms. And in spite of her raging need to be with him, exhaustion claimed her, and she fell asleep in his arms.

Sated and safe tonight because Mason was beside her.

HOURS LATER, MASON WOKE to the sight of sunshine streaming through the window. For the first time in ages, he had a warm body next to him.

He smiled as he glanced down at Cara. She had turned on her side with her back to him, her butt pressed into his groin.

Titillating sensations pulsed through him, the desire he'd denied himself for the past months pooling in his sex. His body hardened, need growing in tandem to the thickening of his length which ached to be inside her.

She sighed softly, and he pulled her closer, then pressed a kiss to her ear while he trailed his other hand over her abdomen. A movement caught him off guard, and he startled, then realized his son was kicking.

A well of emotions mushroomed inside him. His heart churned with instantaneous love. He imagined the little guy's small hands and feet, his face looking up at him and Cara, trusting that they would take care of him.

Lord be with him, he would never let him down. He'd be the father to his son that he'd never had.

Affection for Cara overwhelmed him, and he dropped another kiss into her hair. She stirred in his arms, a slow smile gracing her mouth, reminding him how beautiful she was.

"Good morning," he murmured, because having her in his bed and arms made his heart pound with happiness.

"Good morning to you." She blushed again as she glanced down at her naked belly, and he gently kissed her cheek.

"I felt him kick," he murmured.

She laughed softly. "He's very active in the morning. I think he might be a soccer player."

If he was, he would be there to watch his games.

"Does it hurt when he kicks?"

An expression akin to awe flickered in her eyes. "No, not really. It…reminds me he's alive, that he's a real little man just waiting to come out."

Her tenderly spoken words were so full of love that his heart squeezed. Then her gaze met his, her nipples stiffening as his hand brushed over her heavy breasts, and hunger surged inside him.

He dipped his head and claimed her mouth again, kissing her with all the pent-up hunger he'd lived with since he'd walked out of her life. She kissed him back, her tongue dancing with his, her hands urging him closer.

He wanted to take her there, to have all of her, to promise her that he wouldn't leave her this time.

But how could he do that?

He was a lawman. His job took him across the state, to dangerous places, and forced him to deal with the worst of the worst.

He couldn't expose his son to that kind of danger.

Tension warred with his need for her, and he ordered himself to stop. But his heart and his raging body needed her, and he refused to listen to rational thought.

She moved against him and he cupped her breasts, then lowered his mouth to trace his tongue over one turgid point. She moaned and clung to him, threading her hands into his hair.

He laved one breast, then the other, then suckled one nipple into his mouth. Her leg wound through his, one hand sliding down to cup his backside. His muscles clenched with arousal, his sex throbbing and seeking out her warm center.

But his cell phone jangled, a reminder that he was in the middle of a multiple homicide case.

He wanted to ignore the phone, stall answering that call. Finish what he and Cara had begun.

But his son kicked again, and he couldn't *not* answer it.

Cara and his baby's life depended on him doing his job.

So he gently kissed her again, then reached for his phone. "Detective Blackpaw."

"Detective, it's Reverend Parch."

Mason frowned. "Reverend?"

"Yes…" His voice sounded odd. Troubled. "You need to come out to my church."

Had the reverend decided to spill what he knew? "What's going on?"

"There's a cemetery behind our church. This morning when I arrived, a new grave had been dug."

Mason reached for his shirt. "I take it you didn't have a funeral there yesterday?"

"No," Reverend Parch said. "This one just turned up. And it's different."

"What do you mean?"

"The grave is covered in stones."

Mason cursed. The killer had struck again.

Chapter Fifteen

Something was wrong. When Mason ended the call, he grabbed his jeans and yanked them on, and she reached for her robe.

Disappointment flitted through Cara—she missed the intimacy they had just shared. "What is it?"

"Reverend Parch found a new grave behind the church this morning."

Anger and grief suffused Cara. "Let me get dressed. I'm going with you."

Mason gave a clipped nod and fastened his belt. "I'll make coffee."

"I only have decaf," she said. "I had to give up caffeine during the pregnancy."

He disappeared into the kitchen while she hurried to the bathroom, washed her face and ran a brush through her hair. She threw on slacks and a maternity blouse, then brushed her teeth. Her eyes looked puffy, so she dusted her face with powder, then headed to the kitchen.

Mason was sipping coffee and handed her a cup.

He also had made toast and insisted she eat a slice before they left. Ten minutes later, they were in the car driving toward the church. Mason had brought the bag of evidence the killer had left in her room the night before with him to send to the lab.

Early morning traffic thickened as they entered town, the parking lot of the diner full with the breakfast crowd.

"I phoned Sheriff McRae and Special Agent Whitehead and told them to meet us there," he said. "And I asked Brody to post someone to watch your cabin. If the killer sticks with his pattern, he'll leave another amulet at your place."

Cara shivered at the thought. But if he did show up, maybe Brody's security guard would catch him in the act. "The other burial sites were more deserted areas. It was risky for him to bring the body into town and bury her behind the church."

"Yeah," Mason said, anger lacing his tone. "It's like he's throwing this kill in our faces." Mason quirked his head to the side in thought. "He saw the press conference and it ticked him off."

Cara considered the possibility. "You're right. He's taunting us. He wants us to know he's smarter than we gave him credit for."

"But he doesn't know we're on to him." Mason pulled into the parking lot and came to a stop. "Are you sure you're up for this, Cara?"

She made a sarcastic sound. "No, but I have to do it. I can't let him hurt any more of my patients."

MASON BRACED HIMSELF as he and Cara headed to the front of the church. Cara's phone buzzed, and she glanced at the number, then sighed.

"I need to take this." She connected the call, and he went to greet the sheriff who pulled up behind them. Agent Whitehead arrived on his heels. They discussed the situation for a moment, the mood somber.

Cara joined them. "One of my patients is in labor. I need to go as soon as we're finished here."

Mason nodded, and they entered the building. Reverend Parch greeted them at the door, his expression troubled. "The grave is out back."

"You're the one who found it?" Mason asked.

"Yes. I always stroll through the cemetery early in the morning," Reverend Parch said, earning a questioning look from Cara and making the agent's eyebrows raise.

"Sounds morbid," Mason commented.

The reverend shrugged. "Not at all. I find it peaceful."

"Just show us the grave," Sheriff McRae said in a tone indicating he was less concerned about the preacher's rituals than the fact that another murder had been committed in his town.

Reverend Parch led them through a side door to the cemetery, the morning sun glinting off the headstones. Mason immediately spotted the grave.

It was set apart from the others, the stones marking the fresh mound of dirt.

Cara donned latex gloves while he did the same. Just as before, he took photographs of the stones and their arrangement.

Then he knelt and used a tool from his kit to dig away the dirt. The sheriff helped while Cara and Agent Whitehead watched.

Mason swallowed back revulsion as the young woman's terrified eyes appeared. Then he glanced at Cara. "Was she one of your patients?"

Cara bit down on her lip. "Yes, her name is Angelica Mansfield." She knelt and touched the young woman's face with her hand. "But I don't understand. Angel didn't give her baby up for adoption. She had a miscarriage last month." Her teary eyes met Mason's. "She was devastated over the loss."

Mason's jaw tightened. "Maybe he blames her for losing the child?"

"Or maybe he's escalating and spiraling out of control," Agent Whitehead said. "That means he'll make a mistake and we'll catch him."

Cara stood, her emotions raging. "The question is—how many women have to die first?"

"DOES SHE HAVE FAMILY to notify?" Mason asked.

"A sister, but she lives in Georgia." Cara rubbed her forehead. "I hate to think how that poor woman is going to feel knowing her sister was brutalized like this."

"I'll take care of notifications," Sheriff McRae offered.

"What about the baby's father?" Agent White-head asked.

Cara shook her head. "He was separated from his wife at the time and they'd planned to marry. But when Angel lost the baby he went back to his wife."

Mason muttered an oath beneath his breath. "We need the autopsy to verify cause of death and compare the wounds to the other victims." He turned to the preacher. "Reverend Parch, did you see anyone out here this morning?"

He wrapped his hand around the Bible. "No. I'm afraid not."

Mason folded his arms across his chest. "So you just stumbled on the grave?"

"I told you that I found it during my morning meditation."

"You were alone?"

"Yes." The man stroked the edge of the Bible. "Whoever buried her probably did so during the night."

"What time did you arrive?" Agent Whitehead asked.

"About six a.m. I like to get here early in case some of my parishioners stop by to talk before they go to work."

Mason gave him a skeptical look. Granted they had pegged Morningside as their main suspect, but there was still something fishy about the reverend. Something fake in his eyes.

Secrets.

"Do you know a man named Lapu Morningside?" Mason asked.

Reverend Parch cut his eyes toward the book in his hand. "He has visited our church."

"Did you give him counsel?" Cara asked.

The reverend slanted her a cold look. "You know I can't divulge that any more than you could."

Mason wondered what else he hid behind his religious jargon and the good book.

"If you're covering up a criminal act or if you know where Morningside is and you're not telling us, then I'll arrest you for harboring a criminal and as an accessory to murder."

"Those charges would never stick," Reverend Parch said matter-of-factly.

Agent Whitehead's phone buzzed, and she stepped aside to answer it.

Sheriff McRae cleared his throat. "If Reverend Parch knows something regarding the murder and doesn't report it, he'll have to live with his own conscience."

Mason gestured toward the grave. "Are you going to hide behind your Bible and allow another woman to die?"

For a brief second, pain and grief flickered across the reverend's face. "No. I pray that you find the lost soul who's hurting these women, Detective."

Agent Whitehead returned, her body tense. "We have a lead on Morningside."

Adrenaline surged through Mason. "Then we need to go." He glanced at Cara. "Cara?"

"I have to deliver a baby."

Mason didn't want to leave her alone for a second. "It's not safe for you at the clinic."

"I'm not shutting down my practice, Mason. My patient is in labor."

"I'll send my deputy over to watch the place," Sheriff McRae offered.

An uneasy feeling nagged at Mason. A vision of Cara lying in bed this morning, naked, her body pressed into his, sent a surge of protective instincts through him.

More than anything he wanted to catch this killer. And Cara wouldn't be safe until he did.

"A caller claims he saw Morningside at a gas station between here and San Antonio," Agent Whitehead cut in. "It sounds like he's on the run."

Mason shifted. If Morningside was out of town, Cara would be safe. Besides, he'd had security measures installed at the clinic, and the deputy would be there.

"All right, I'll drop you, Cara." He turned to the agent. "Follow me and then we'll ride together."

"I'll stay here and wait on the crime scene techs and see that our victim is transported to the ME's office," Sheriff McRae said.

Mason jangled his car keys. "Call your deputy now and tell him to meet us at the Winchester clinic."

McRae agreed, and he and Cara and the agent hurried to their cars. But as Mason drove to the Winchester clinic, his nerves were on edge.

He hoped to hell this caller was right, and that they found Morningside.

He wanted Cara safe and back in bed with him like they were this morning.

CARA CLENCHED HER TEETH as Mason drove her to the clinic. How would Isabella Morningside feel if her ex-husband was the serial killer? What if he came after her? Killing her might be his end game.

She had to warn Isabella and her other patients.

By the time they arrived, the deputy was waiting.

Mason introduced himself. "Don't leave this place for a moment," he told the deputy. "We think Morningside left town, but he might circle back and come after Dr. Winchester."

The deputy's expression indicated he understood the seriousness of the situation. "I'll make sure she's safe."

Mason shook his hand, then gave Cara one more look. She memorized his face, his eyes, knew that he couldn't make promises he couldn't keep.

But she wanted him to promise that he'd come back to her alive.

"Dr. Winchester," Sherese said as she met her at the door. "Hurry, Ann is at nine centimeters!"

Cara took a deep breath, then waved to Mason

and dashed inside. Three other patients sat in the waiting room, one a woman with a young boy who looked as if he had a bad cough. The other two were routine pregnancy checks.

"I'll be with you all as soon as I can," she said as she passed them and went to wash her hands and suit up.

Sherese followed her, filling her in. "Her water broke at six a.m., then the contractions started. I've prepped her for an epidural but I think it's too late."

Cara nodded, and gripped Sherese's hands. "Listen, Sherese. Another woman was murdered last night by this navel fetish killer. The police think it was Isabella Morningside's ex-husband. Call her and warn her to go a friend's house and stay there. Then call all my patients who chose adoption, and warn them that my files have been compromised and that they need to be vigilant about not being alone."

"I'll get right on it," Sherese said. "Do you want me to tell them it's Morningside?"

"No," Cara said. "We can't be sure. Just warn them to be careful."

Sherese hurried back to the front desk, and Cara slipped in to the delivery room. Ann Martin, her eighteen-year-old patient, looked up at her with panicked eyes. Her mother stood beside her, wiping her face with a cloth.

"Help me, Dr. Winchester," Ann screeched. "The baby's coming."

Cara gave the young girl's mother a reassuring smile. "Then let's get your little girl here."

She pulled on gloves, then examined Ann. "You're right," she said with another smile. "This baby is ready to meet her mother."

Another contraction seized her, and Ann clenched the bed rail. "Breathe, honey," her mother said.

The mother gripped her daughter's hands, and Cara patted Ann's arm. "Good job. Now I'm going to need you to push."

Sweat beaded Ann's face and neck, and she choked on a sob as she clutched the bed, lifted herself to a half sitting position and pushed.

"She's crowning now, I see her head," Cara said. "Hang on a minute, sugar."

The young girl wiped at tears. "Is she okay?"

"Everything's fine," Cara said, although the cord was wrapped around the baby's neck, and she had to unwind it before Ann pushed her the rest of the way out. Each contraction was choking the infant.

"Doctor?" Ann's mother said with a note of panic in her voice as another contraction squeezed Ann's abdomen.

"One minute, then we'll push her out." Cara carefully unwound the cord, then looked up at Ann. "Okay, now push!"

Another big push and the baby slid into Cara's hands. She caught her and turned her over, slowly massaging her chest until a second later, the baby cried out.

"She's perfect, ten fingers, ten toes!" Cara said triumphantly.

Ann and her mother cried and hugged each other while Cara cleaned the baby and checked her Apgar score. She cut the cord, then wrapped the squealing little girl in a blanket and eased her into her mother's arms.

"She's beautiful," Ann whispered.

"My little angel," her mother cried.

The next half hour was hectic as Cara finished caring for Ann. "I'm going to send you to the hospital for the night," Cara said. "Just to make sure all the necessary tests are run for the baby."

Ann looked frightened for a moment, but Cara assured her that it was routine. She darted into the front room and phoned the ambulance.

She had another patient to see so she left Ann and her mother waiting for the ambulance while she examined the little boy and gave him an antibiotic, then walked them to the front.

A car alarm sounded down the street, and Cara tensed.

The deputy frowned. "I'll check it out."

Cara nodded, and he jogged down the street while she headed to the next exam room.

The ambulance arrived and Sherese sent the medics to transport Ann and the baby. Just as they were carrying her out, a sound echoed from the side of the building. A window shattered.

Cara frowned and rushed to see what had happened, then stared in horror as she spotted a pipe bomb on the floor.

The bomb was going to explode any second.

Chapter Sixteen

Mason parked at the gas station where the attendant had spotted Morningside, and he and Agent White-field scanned the premises as they entered. A few customers were in the store browsing for snacks, coffee and drinks.

A young man wearing dreadlocks with a tattoo of a snake on his arm worked the register. "My name is Sheriff Blackpaw and this is Special Agent White-head of the FBI. Are you the person who called in about the investigation?"

The boy inched his shoulders up as if he was impressed by their credentials. "Yeah."

"What's your name?" Agent Whitehead asked.

"Tray Vaughn," the boy said.

Mason showed him a printout with Morningside's photo on it. "Is this the man you saw, Tray?"

Tray's brows furrowed. "He don't look like that."

"This is his military photo," Mason explained. "His hair is longer now, and he was probably wearing civilian clothes."

"Could be. He has a scar above his eye," the boy said.

Mason glanced at Agent Whitehead and she nodded. "Shrapnel."

"What time did he stop by?"

"Late last night. I close up so it was around midnight."

"What did he say when he came in?" Mason asked.

"Nothing much," Tray said. "He bought some razors and shaving cream, water, and some cans of food. Oh, and electrical tape."

Hmm, the shaving cream, razors, food sounded like he might be planning to camp or hide out for a while. But the electrical tape—that worried him. "Did he say where he was going?"

"Naw." The boy glanced at the door as a heavyset Hispanic man entered. "But he bought a map of the state. And he asked me if there was any rental cabins nearby."

Mason's interest perked up. "Are there?"

The boy nodded. "Out on the old state road near Hawk's Crossing."

"Did you notice if he had a weapon with him?" Agent Whitehead asked.

"Didn't see no gun."

"How about a knife?" Mason asked. He removed another flier with a photo of the buffalo skinner and showed it to the kid. "Maybe one that looked like this."

Tray shook his head. "Didn't see one, but he had on a big jacket. Could have hid it under it."

Mason noticed the security camera above the cash register and another one in the back corner. "Can I look at the security footage?"

The boy blushed. "Cameras don't work. Owner, that'd be Mr. Darnell, he put 'em up just to scare off shoplifters."

Mason muttered a silent curse. What use was security if it wasn't armed?

The heavyset man approached with a six-pack of beer while two teenagers lined up behind him with snacks.

"One more thing," Mason said. "What kind of car was he driving?"

"Drove an old Jeep. Black, I think it was."

The man behind him cleared his throat. "Can we hurry it up? I got to get back to the job."

Mason cut him a scathing look then flashed his badge and gestured toward the beer. "Taking that to work with you?"

The man sneered at him, but held up a hand indicating he would wait.

"Draw me a map to this place called Hawk's Crossing," Mason said.

The boy turned the sketch of the knife over and scribbled a crude map and directions on the back. Mason thanked him, and he and the agent left.

"I hope to hell he's there," Mason said.

"We'll find him," Agent Whitehead assured him.

Mason bit back a sarcastic comment. This was only a case to her.

To him, it was personal. Extremely personal.

SMOKE BILLOWED UPWARD, a ticking sound exploding in Cara's ears. Dear God, the pipe bomb was going to blow.

She raced toward the reception area and shouted at Sherese. "There's a pipe bomb inside the clinic. Hurry, get everyone out!"

The paramedics jumped into motion, rushing Ann, her mother and the baby outside. Sherese took one of the female patients by the arm, while Cara raced to the other, her bulk making it difficult to move as fast as she wanted.

Connie, the woman with Sherese, started crying, but Sherese guided her to the door. "Come on, honey, let's go outside. We have to save your baby."

Bailey, the second woman, stood, eyes wide with horror. "What's happening, Dr. Winchester?"

"I'll explain later, let's go." She helped Bailey from the waiting area to the door. Behind her, the smoke grew thicker.

One of the paramedics rushed back to help her.

"Get them as far away from the building as possible," Cara ordered.

He helped Bailey while the other medic quickly loaded Ann, the baby and her mother into the ambulance.

"Is anyone else inside?" the second medic asked.

"No," Cara said. "Make sure the patients are okay while I call 911."

The medics and Sherese moved the two pregnant women near the ambulance, then suddenly the bomb exploded.

Smoke filled the air, glass shattered and the right side of the women's pavilion burst into flames.

Cara was so close to the door that the impact threw her to the ground.

She tasted dirt and felt blood trickle down her cheek as she collapsed into the grass.

MASON FOLLOWED THE crude map, veering onto the side roads leading deeper into the wilderness.

Morningside had his little shopping spree late last night. Which meant he was hours ahead of them.

And that they could be on a wild goose chase.

Still, they couldn't afford not to follow up on the lead. Prairie land stretched before him, cacti, mesquites, scrub brush and patches of wildlife that normally he found peaceful.

Now they represented places to hide.

"Turn on that road," Agent Whitehead said as she studied the map. "It should be a few miles down there."

Mason turned on to the dirt road, the car bouncing over potholes. Ahead vultures soared above, reminding him of the first body he'd found. God, he hoped Morningside didn't have another victim out here now.

A tree had fallen across the road forcing him to slam on the brakes.

"How did Morningside get past this?" Agent Whitehead asked.

"Maybe he's the one that put it down, a way to keep anyone from coming farther."

Agent Whitehead twisted her hair into a knot on the back of her head. "What do we do now?"

"Hike in." Mason cut the engine and climbed out. Agent Whitehead followed, and they headed in the direction of the vultures.

The sound of birds cawing and animals skittering through the woods echoed around them, an occasional branch crackling from the wind.

He approached the patch of brush where the vultures hovered, then breathed a sigh of relief when he realized that it was a carcass of a deer on the ground, not another woman's body.

"That's nasty," Agent Whitehead said, her nose curling up.

"Better an animal than a human." Mason studied the map again, then strode to the right. They climbed a small hill and came to a clearing and a creek, then he followed the creek to the east.

The sound of the water gurgling should have been comforting, but with each step he took, he sensed they were walking into a trap.

Agent Whitehead wiped her forehead with the back of her hand. "Look, there's a cabin."

Miles spotted it at the same time she did. "Let's

go." Gravel skidded beneath his boots as he descended the hill.

"Dammit," she said. "I should have brought my hiking boots."

He didn't bother to comment. The feds and their stuffy suits got on his nerves, but so far she had been decent to work with. At least she wasn't a whiner and hadn't complained about the bugs that swarmed them as they walked.

Mason paused behind a tree and studied the cabin, and the agent did the same.

"See any movement?" he asked.

She shook her head no. "No Jeep, either."

"He may already be gone."

"Only one way to find out."

He nodded, then gritted his teeth as they slid the rest of the way down the hill. He used the bushes to hide as they approached, then snuck up to the window and peered inside. The cabin looked rustic and deserted, the interior sparsely furnished. Birds had made a nest on the porch, and it looked as if squirrels had chewed a hole in the roof edge.

He motioned for the agent to check the front while he made his way around back. He checked the side window and spotted a bed in one room and a small dingy bathroom beside it. No one was inside.

He hesitated, then listened for sounds, but the place was eerily quiet.

Frustration knotted his belly as he crept around

to the back, then jiggled the door. It swung open, a stench hitting him.

Praying it wasn't a body, he wielded his gun and inched inside. The kitchen was overflowing with discarded fast food wrappers and rotting food, the source of the smell. Rat droppings littered the floor in front of the sink. An old Formica table was covered in stuff, but he didn't take time to examine it. He had to make sure the house was clear.

He inched into the room, taking cover behind the doorway as he checked the living room, but it was empty. So were the bedrooms.

He opened the front door and waved Agent Whitehead in. "No one here."

She muttered a sound of frustration.

"Look for anything that might tell us where he went."

She nodded and searched the den while he strode back to the kitchen. His gut clenched at the sight of the items on the table.

Steel piping. Electrical tape. And chemicals. Black powder to be exact.

All the materials needed to make a pipe bomb.

Dear God. What did he plan to do with it?

The floor creaked, and Mason froze, jerking his head around to make sure Morningside hadn't been hiding out.

But Agent Whitehead stood at the doorway, her expression disturbed. "The sheriff just called."

Mason braced himself. "What happened?"

"A bomb just exploded at the Winchester Clinic."

Mason's lung squeezed for air. God, no...

"Were there injuries?" he asked in a choked voice.

"No, the fire department is there now."

"I have to go."

"What about this evidence?" Agent Whitehead asked.

He was so scared his vision blurred. "I'll send someone back for it. I have to get to the clinic."

Agent Whitehead frowned, but he ignored her and headed for the door.

"The sheriff is there," Agent Whitehead said. "We have to process the house."

Mason glared at her. "You stay. I'll send someone back for you."

"I don't understand—"

He didn't care if she understood or not. Cara and his baby could have died.

He had to see them for himself to make sure they were all right.

Sirens rent the air, and another ambulance careened to a stop. Cara peeled herself from the ground, her ears ringing, and swayed as she headed toward Sherese.

The fire engine roared up, firemen jumping down, unrolling hoses at lightning speed as they began to douse the flames.

Sherese caught her. "Cara, God, are you all right?"

She nodded, although she felt dizzy. "The patients…"

"They're all okay," Sherese said. "But I'm not so sure about you. You look pale, and you're bleeding."

A female paramedic rushed toward them. "Come on, my name is Billy Jo, sit down."

"This is Dr. Winchester," Sherese told the young woman.

Billy Jo smiled, her expression calm as she led Cara to a second ambulance that had arrived. A male medic had opened up the back, and they helped Cara sit on the edge.

"I'm fine," Cara insisted. "I just want to make sure my patients are okay."

"The first ambulance took Ann and her little girl to the hospital," Sherese assured her. "And the others are safe."

"Now let's make sure your baby didn't suffer." Billy Jo cleaned the blood off Cara's cheek. "Looks like a cut from a piece of glass. But it's not deep so you shouldn't need stitches. Were you hit anywhere else?"

Cara shook her head. "No, the impact threw me to the ground, but I'm fine."

Sherese squeezed her hand. "Cara, if this were one of your patients, you'd insist they be examined, so stop being so stubborn."

Cara jerked her head toward her friend, for the first time since she'd seen that pipe bomb, aware how terrifying it had been for Sherese. Yet Sherese had calmly helped the patients to safety.

"I'm sorry," she said, giving Sherese an apologetic smile.

Sherese nodded. "I know, you're used to being the boss, but this time I am."

Cara laughed, the tension dissipating, then allowed the medic to examine her.

"Your blood pressure's slightly elevated," Billy Jo said.

"Understandable considering the circumstances," Cara said, unconcerned.

Billy Jo listened to the baby's heartbeat. "Sounds strong," the medic said. "Do you have pain anywhere?"

"My ears were ringing a little, but it's subsiding," Cara said.

"You're dizzy?"

"Just shaken," Cara said. "But I'm feeling better now."

"Do you want to go in for observation?" Billy Jo asked.

Cara shook her head. "I know the signs. If I have pain or go into labor, I'll call 911 myself."

Suddenly a news van pulled up, and the reporter who'd interviewed Agent Whitehead, Dayna Lipton, slid from the car and headed toward her, mic in hand, a cameraman on her heels.

"Dr. Winchester," she called as she approached. "Can you tell us what happened here?"

Cara hated news coverage, but she couldn't avoid it. A crowd was forming around the building already, other storeowners and citizens running to see the fire. "Someone threw a pipe bomb into the clinic. Thankfully all of our patients and staff escaped unharmed."

"Do you think the man the FBI is looking for, the Navel Fetish killer, is responsible?"

Cara hadn't had time to think about it, but it was possible. "I don't know," she said honestly.

"The police are searching for a man named Lapu Morningside as a person of interest. Can you comment on that?"

"I'm not at liberty to discuss the investigation," she said.

Still, she was tired of hiding and feeling guilty for the crimes this maniac was committing. So she made a snap decision.

She turned back to the camera, a challenge in her eyes. "I'd like to speak to the man who did this directly. It's obvious you have a vendetta against me. So leave my patients alone. If you want me, then come after me. There's no reason to hurt anyone else."

When she glanced up, she spotted Mason. He must have driven up and come through the crowd. And he'd obviously heard her. Rage burned in his eyes as he stalked toward her and pushed away the camera. "Get out of here now," he snapped at Dayna. "Let the officers and firefighters do their jobs."

Dayna smiled at him, though, as if she'd gotten what she wanted, then she and the cameraman began interviewing bystanders.

Mason gripped her arm. "What the hell are you doing, Cara?"

"I'm trying to end this." She gestured toward the clinic. The fire department had managed to save half of it, but the other half of the women's pavilion lay in ruins, the ashes smoldering, smoke still swirling in the air.

"For God's sake, Mason, he could have hurt dozens of innocent people today. And not just women, but children, and Sherese." She heaved a breath. "If we have to set a trap to catch him, then let's do it. I can't live with any more deaths on my conscience."

HE STOOD ON THE EDGE of the crowd, smiling as he watched the good doctor lose her cool. She had a temper, that one did.

Oh, it would make it so much more fun when he finally trapped her.

But this fire, the bomb…they were fools if they thought it was his style. Idiots.

Blackpaw moved closer to the doctor, and he watched as the detective put a protective arm around her.

Laughter bubbled in his throat and threatened to erupt, but he stifled it. He couldn't draw attention to himself.

Not yet.

But, oh, he liked watching them sweat and chase their tails.

And what sweet pleasure to know that Blackpaw would suffer as well as his lover when Dr. Winchester finally got what was coming to her.

Chapter Seventeen

Mason clenched his teeth to control his anger. "My God, what are you doing? You can't invite this maniac to come after you."

"He's going to sooner or later," Cara said, a dozen emotions sizzling in her eyes. "We might as well take charge. Then maybe we can stop him from hurting anyone else."

"But what about you?" His voice cracked as he glanced down at her belly. "What about our son? You don't mind putting him at risk?"

Cara pinned him with an angry look. "Of course I mind, but I don't have a choice. I'm already a target, so let's just skip the extra victims and force him to come after the person he really wants."

For a tense heartbeat, they stared at each other, the uncertainty, anger and fear palpable. On some level, Mason was aware that the sheriff had approached, that that damn reporter was still around.

Hell, Morningside might even be in the crowd watching.

He muttered a string of expletives.

Then he released his hold on Cara and swung around. He'd been such a fool, reacting on emotions and terror for Cara and his baby, that he had neglected the obvious.

Of course, Morningside was somewhere nearby watching.

It was typical of a criminal, especially one who made a public statement like a bombing. He took pleasure in watching the police and emergency workers scurry around.

Reveled in the fear and chaos he'd caused.

And *he* had played into the madman's hands.

Instead of approaching the scene like a cop, he'd been too damn out of his mind with worry over Cara and the baby to do his job.

He'd also tipped his hand. Given away the fact that this case was personal to him.

A rookie mistake.

And one that could not only get him killed, but endanger Cara and his child even more.

He visually swept the crowd, scanning the street. A group of teens, two elderly women, a couple with their baby in a stroller, three truck drivers he recognized from the diner, and a group of onlookers standing with Reverend Parch.

A movement caught his eye, and he swung to the left and noticed a figure huddled in a hoodie walking briskly the other way.

"Stay here, Cara," Mason said. "I'll be back."

Then he took off through the crowd. Suddenly the figure pivoted and looked straight at him.

Mason's heart raced as he looked into the vacant eyes of Morningside.

For God's sake. He had been there. Had set that bomb and was walking away as if nothing had happened.

Mason pulled his gun, maneuvered through the group of churchgoers, increasing his pace as Morningside veered into the alley.

Mason broke into a jog, then turned down the alley, but the man had disappeared. Adrenaline kicked in. He couldn't have gotten too far.

He glanced left then right, then thought he detected movement down the street. More run-down buildings stood like festering sores in the deserted alley, another reminder that Cara's clinic wasn't in the best part of town. But he bypassed them, then thought he spotted Morningside ahead.

Running now, he crossed the intersection, racing down the street. The man disappeared around the corner, then Mason chased him through a low-income housing project. Clothes flapped on a clothesline, and he shoved sheets aside as he sprinted through the yard. A dog barked nearby, another one running into the alley.

"Whoa, guys," he said, holding up his hand to calm them.

The larger one, a Doberman, bared his teeth and growled and the other, a shepherd mix, lunged at him. "Hey, guys, I'm not going to hurt you," Mason murmured.

A chuffy guy with baggy clothes and eyes that looked glassy from drugs stepped into the yard.

"I'm a detective," Mason said. "Call off your dogs."

"Huh?"

Frustration made Mason curse. "Call them off or I'll raid your place and throw you in jail."

The guy threw up his hand in submission, then whistled, and the dogs trotted to him and plopped down at his feet.

Mason took off running, but by the time he made it past the housing development, Morningside had disappeared.

He leaned over with his hands on his knees and heaved a breath. Dammit to hell.

The man had escaped.

And after Cara's challenge, he would come after her. The only question was when and where he would strike?

CARA MADE SURE her patients were calm enough to drive home, then warned them that the attack was personal against her, to be on guard until the Navel Fetish killer was caught.

"Call me if you start having contractions or any problems," she said. Both women had two months before they were due, so hopefully their pregnancies hadn't been jeopardized by the day's trauma.

Mason looked stark and fierce against the fading sunset as he appeared from the alley and headed toward her. His face was set in stone, sweat beading on his brow. He'd obviously been chasing Morningside, but his bleak expression indicated that he'd lost him.

He was still furious at her, as well.

But she didn't intend to back down. She wanted this craziness to end so she and her patients could be safe again.

Cara turned to Sherese. "Thanks for all your help, now go home, sweetie."

Sherese shook her head. "I have to get those files so I can finish making those phone calls tonight."

Sherese had already done so much that Cara was tempted to relieve her of the task, but in light of the bombing, the women had to be warned.

"I'll email you the list from my home computer," Cara said. "It'll be a while before it's safe to go back inside."

"What about our patients?" Sherese asked.

"For now, cancel your appointments," Mason cut in as he came to an abrupt stop in front of her.

"Mason, I can't do that. This is a medical clinic. Babies won't stop being born just because there's trouble."

"Then refer the ones who need immediate care to the hospital," he said emphatically. "You're not coming back here until this maniac is caught."

Cara reluctantly agreed. One of the firefighters

walked toward them and introduced himself as Ben Filmore.

"We found evidence of arson," Filmore said. "There were pieces of steel piping and traces of black powder at the point of origin."

"I found both substances at the cabin where we tracked Morningside," Mason said. "Special Agent Whitehead stayed back to wait on a crime unit to process the scene and gather the evidence."

Cara folded her arms across her middle. That evidence definitely pointed to Morningside as the bomber. She had only met the man once and tried to remember what he looked like. He was part Comanche like Mason, but his features weren't as prominent. When she'd seen him, he had scraggly brown hair and a beard and a dozen scars on his arms and face. That had been shortly after he returned from Afghanistan where he'd been a prisoner of war for three months. No telling what brutalities he'd suffered.

Enough to make him bomb her clinic where innocent women and children could have been killed? If only he'd gotten psychiatric help like Isabella had begged him to do.

"When can we get back inside?" Cara asked him.

"Not for a while, ma'am. Even the parts of the clinic that weren't destroyed by the fire have smoke and water damage."

Disappointment and frustration filled Cara. All

she wanted to do was help people but this man was endangering them.

"I'll ask the sheriff to post a couple of men here round the clock," Filmore said. "We'll confiscate all your drugs and equipment that can be salvaged and put it all into storage."

"Thanks. We can't have looters trying to steal the equipment or medication." Although worry nagged at her. How would she rebuild? Even with insurance, it would take time and would be costly to replace laboratory equipment and supplies. They'd had so many donations to get them started, done fund-raising…

They would have to do it all over again. But she wouldn't let this man win and shut her down.

Sherese hugged her goodbye and hurried to her car, and Cara sighed with fatigue.

"Come on, Cara," Mason said. "I'm driving you home. You look beat."

A weariness settled over Cara. "I hate to leave the clinic like this."

"The sheriff will make sure it's secure," he said. "You need to rest. Isn't that what you'd tell your patients in this situation?"

Cara glared at him, but she could hardly argue with that. "Fine."

Although how could she rest knowing Morningside was still out there? That he might come after her tonight?

That he might be stalking another victim to make her pay for challenging him in front of the press?

MASON STOPPED BY the dining hall on the BBL to pick up dinner plates for them. Ms. Ellen packed pieces of her special coconut cream pie for dessert while Cara spoke to Jordan and Kim to make sure the boys who'd been with Mason when he'd discovered Nellie Thompson's body weren't traumatized.

"Doc Winchester okay?" Ms. Ellen asked. "I saw her on the TV and she looked exhausted."

"That's why I wanted dinner for her. Then I'm going to make sure she rests tonight."

"You call me if she go into labor," Ms. Ellen said. "I ain't no doctor but I delivered a young'un or two myself."

Mason smiled at the kind woman. Johnny Long had brought her to the BBL and everyone adored her. She was also the best cook he'd ever met.

He patted her shoulder. "Thanks, that's a relief. I don't know what I'd do if I had to deliver the baby myself."

Ms. Ellen laughed and Brody approached. "I saw the news about the fire in town. Thank God no one was hurt."

"Yeah, it could have been worse," Mason said. Except Cara's quick courage and dedication had saved everyone inside. She was always taking care of everyone else.

But who took care of her?

He would tonight.

"That was a pretty bold move challenging Morningside," Brody said.

"Don't remind me," Mason growled.

"My security team will be on guard tonight," Brody said. "I'll also have one nearby Cara's place."

"I'm staying there until this guy is caught," Mason assured him. "He'll have to kill me to get to her and that baby."

Brody gave him an understanding look, and Mason thanked him then walked over to Cara. "You ready?"

She rubbed at her lower back. "Yes."

A silence fell between them as they drove to her cabin. When they arrived, Mason insisted she stay in the car until he searched the rooms. But it was clear, so she came in and he set their plates at the table.

"Eat," he said, his temper still fuming at the fact that she'd practically invited Morningside to come after her.

His cell phone buzzed, and he checked the number. "It's Agent Whitehead. I'd better get it."

Cara nodded, then sat down to eat.

He stepped onto the porch and scanned the property as he connected the call. "Blackpaw."

"It's Agent Whitehead," she said. "The crime unit collected everything at the cabin and are processing it now. How are things there?"

"We're back at Cara's." He explained the fire chief's findings.

"So Morningside built the bomb at the cabin," Agent Whitehead said. "Then he tossed it in the clinic and ran."

"He was in the crowd watching the pandemonium," Mason said through gritted teeth.

"That fits the profile," she said. "But there's something that's bothering me about all this."

Mason tensed. "What?"

"It's about Cara's comment. She challenged him to come after her, the source of his rage. It's true that Morningside blames her for his wife's decision to leave him, but ultimately he's furious at his wife."

The hair on the back of Mason's neck bristled. "So you think he may go after his wife?"

"It's possible," Agent Whitehead said. "We know he's unstable. We have to cover all bases."

"You're right," Mason said. "But I'm not leaving Cara."

"I understand," Agent Whitehead said. "I'm on my way to the ex-wife's. I'll stay with her tonight in case he shows there."

"Good, you can relieve Liam Runninghorse so he can help search the res." Mason disconnected, then went back inside to check on Cara. She had eaten half of her dinner, but her eyelids looked heavy.

She looked so sweet and vulnerable that he didn't have the heart to fuss at her. "Go get some rest, Cara." He took her arm and helped her up. She gave him a grateful smile, but fatigue lined her face as she walked into the bedroom.

The memory of her lying naked in his arms the night before returned to taunt him. Desire bolted through him. He wanted to strip his clothes, crawl into bed with her and hold her again until she fell asleep against him.

But he couldn't allow himself that luxury. Tonight he wasn't Cara's lover or the baby's father.

He was a cop tracking down a sadistic killer.

And that meant staying alert so he could protect Cara and his son.

ONE LAST NAME ON his list before he went after the good doctor.

He slid his fingers over the knife at his waist, then studied the tiny house where she lived. He'd been watching her for days now, knew her routine.

She never saw her little boy because she slept during the day so she could work all night. She let her parents raise the baby so she could come and go as she wanted.

He picked the lock on the back door, slipped into her house, tiptoed through the living room and made his way to her bedroom. Careful not to touch anything, he stretched out on her plush white comforter to wait for her.

She had his people's blood in her child's veins.

Yet she had defied their upbringing.

And now she had to pay for her mistake.

Chapter Eighteen

Cara didn't think she could sleep, but she faded the moment her head hit the pillow. Hours later, she stirred to a dim streak of light poking through the storm clouds outside. She rolled over, disappointed that Mason hadn't joined her.

The memory of him in her bed made her ache for him.

She pushed herself up, slipped on her robe, and walked to the den. But Mason wasn't in the room. She glanced through the window and saw him on her porch drinking coffee, his body tense, his jaw set.

She opened the door and stepped outside. "Have you been out here all night?"

He shook his head. "Just stepped out to have some coffee."

"You didn't sleep?" Cara asked.

"Don't worry about me, Cara. I'll sleep when Morningside is caught."

Cara's phone jangled, and she rushed to answer it

in case it was an emergency. But it was Kim. "Cara, a bunch of boys are complaining of a rash. We think it's poison ivy. Would you mind taking a look?"

"Let me throw on some clothes and I'll be right over."

Mason had followed her inside. "What was that about?"

"Nothing serious, just a group of the campers with poison ivy. I told Kim I'd meet her at the main house clinic."

Mason nodded, then went back outside to stand watch. She made a cup of tea, then dressed while she drank it, and ate a piece of toast.

Mason followed her to the BBL main house and waited outside while she examined the boys.

Five campers were hunched on the cots with red blotches on their faces and arms, their eyes puffy as they twitched and clawed at the patches of irritated skin.

"You poor guys," she said softly. "We're going to make you feel better soon."

Mason knocked on the door and poked his head inside. "Cara?"

The gruff tone of his voice indicated something was wrong.

"Excuse me, boys, I'll be right back."

She patted the youngest boy's shoulder then waddled to the door. "What's wrong?"

"Liam Runninghorse just called. There's trouble at the reservation."

Panic caught in Cara's throat. "Isabella?"

"Morningside got the drop on the agent and has Isabella. I have to go."

"Wait a minute, and I'll go with you."

"Hell, no," Mason said. "You're staying here where you'll be safe. I'll call you when we have him in custody."

Fear clawed at Cara, and she clutched Mason's arm. She wanted to beg him not to go, but she knew that would be futile. No one was safe until Morningside was in jail. And she couldn't stand it if he killed Isabella.

"Mason, please be careful." She pulled his hand to her stomach. "Your son needs you."

His gaze latched with hers, emotions darkening the hues. But a smile twitched at his mouth, then he kissed her and raced out the door.

MASON FLEW ONTO the reservation, adrenaline pumping through him as he parked near Isabella Morningside's hogan. Apparently the agent's instincts had been right. The man had come after his wife.

By the time he arrived, Runninghorse and Chief Pann were outside stationed behind their vehicles along with Carter Flagstone and Sadie Whitefeather.

Sadie was tending to Agent Whitehead who was propped against a tree a few feet away. He crossed the grass to her and noted blood on the back of her head. Sadie was cleaning it with gauze.

"What happened?" he asked.

Agent Whitehead scowled. She was obviously beating herself up over what happened. "I heard a noise and stepped outside to check it out. Bastard hit me from behind with a two by four. I blacked out."

"You're sure he has Isabella in there?"

She nodded in disgust. "I woke up in the dirt, tied to a post. I heard Isabella crying."

Mason frowned. At least the man hadn't killed the agent.

Why exactly had he spared her?

Carter hovered by Sadie, on guard himself, as Liam joined them.

"So far, we've managed to keep this quiet," Liam said. "But if word leaks, we'll have rubberneckers flocking."

"If you see anyone, make them stay back," Mason said. "The last thing we want is to have the press out here or another innocent hurt while we try to arrest Morningside."

"So how do you suggest we handle this?" Chief Pann asked.

Liam propped one hand across the tree as he studied the house. "Should we call in a hostage negotiator?"

"There's no time," Mason said. "He's part Indian, so am I. Get me a bullhorn and I'll talk to him."

Agent Whitehead pushed Sadie's hands away and wrangled to her feet while Chief Pann rushed to his SUV.

"Remember the profile, detective. He was in the

army, has PTSD," Agent Whitehead said. "He's probably suffering from nightmares, lack of sleep, depression. A sense of hopelessness." She pulled her gun from inside her jacket. "He may be having flashbacks, even delusions, and be disoriented."

"You mean he may not realize what he's doing or where he is?"

She shrugged. "In severe cases, the person believes he's still in the middle of combat, and sees everyone else as the enemy. That may have been the reason he bombed the Winchester Clinic."

Mason wanted to have sympathy for the guy, but he had hurt too many people for him to do so. Morningside had to be stopped.

Chief Pann returned with a bullhorn and ear mics for each of them so they could communicate. Mason settled his mic in his ear, gripped the bullhorn with one hand, then gestured toward the agent and Liam. "Go around the house and look in the windows. See if you can find out what room they're in. But nobody takes a shot without clearing it with me." He turned to Carter. "Make sure Sadie stays back and watch out in case any other civilians show up."

They all gave nods of agreement, and Carter ushered Sadie behind the chief's SUV while he inched toward the house.

"Morningside, it's Detective Mason Blackpaw. We need to talk."

"Get out of here!" Morningside shouted. "This is my land, my house."

"That may be true," Mason said, using a calm voice. "And I understand that you're having a hard time, Lapu. That the army did something to you and you need help."

"What do you know?" Morningside bellowed. "You weren't there."

"No, but I understand you were in combat, that you suffered," he said. "That you were held prisoner. That had to be tough."

A tense silence ensued. "I was a soldier, that's what I was trained for."

"But even soldiers crack under torture," Mason said. "And then you came back home and thought you were free, but you couldn't escape it, could you? The nightmares started, you couldn't sleep."

"No, I couldn't," Morningside said, his voice edged with pain. "But I got through prison 'cause I thought my wife was here waiting on me. Only she wasn't."

"Your wife, Isabella, is she all right in there?" Mason asked. "Because I know you really love her and don't want to hurt her."

"Shut up about my wife. She didn't understand."

"How could she?" Mason asked. "She wasn't there, but maybe you can tell her. You two can sit down and talk. She is willing to talk, aren't you, Isabella?"

"Yes," the woman cried.

Mason sighed in relief. At least she was still alive.

"It's too late for talking," Morningside said. "Too late for us."

"No, it's not too late," Mason said. "Not too late to get help."

"You're lying," Morningside yelled. "Just like they did over there. You're the enemy, all of you are."

"That's not true," Mason said, sensing he was losing the man. "The enemy is in your head, Lapu, but I can help you make those voices go away. Make those nightmares fade."

Suddenly the sound of a window crashing rent the air, and Mason saw a figure at the front window, kneeling, a shot gun poking through the shattered glass.

"Stay back, Blackpaw. I told you it's too late. This is between me and my wife."

Mason's hand slid down to his gun. His job was to protect innocents, and he couldn't let the man kill Isabella.

So he stepped closer and prayed that today was not the day he'd lose his life to the job.

CARA WAS SO DISTRACTED with worry over Mason that she could hardly focus on the kids.

"It itches," ten-year-old Buddy said as he clawed at his stomach.

"I know, sweetie," Cara said. "But try not to scratch." She rubbed lotion on the patches of infected red skin.

Then she gestured to the extra bottles on the counter and addressed the counselor in charge of the group. "Take these back to the cabin and keep the boys coated. Hopefully, they'll feel better soon. Meanwhile keep them occupied so they won't scratch so much."

The counselor rolled her eyes as if that was an impossibility and she was ridiculous to even suggest it. Cara smiled, knowing the girl was right, but she'd done all she could do. Her phone jangled, and she stepped aside to answer it, waving to the boys as they filed out.

"Dr. Winchester."

"It's Sherese, Cara. Listen, I checked the messages on the clinic's service, and Delia Nez phoned that she's worried about her little boy. She said her car died so she can't bring him in and wanted to know if you could stop by and take a look at him."

"I'm on my way," Cara said.

She went to tell Brody, but he was leading a riding session with Johnny Long and Brandon Woodstock, so she left a message explaining that she had a house call.

Then she grabbed her purse and headed to her car. She punched Delia's number as she started the engine, but it rang several times, worrying her more. She wished she'd given Sherese more information.

Her mind turned to Mason and the fact that Morningside might hurt Isabella as she left the BBL. Had Mason been able to get there before something terrible happened? Had he convinced Morningside to accept help?

Maybe if she'd gone with him, she could have helped somehow?

Worry gnawed at her.

Mason was such a hero he might barge in to save Isabella and end up getting shot himself.

Her lungs fought for air at the thought. No… Mason had to be okay. Her son needed him.

She needed him.

Her belly tightened as if her baby sensed her anxiety, and she forced herself to breathe slowly in and out. For a brief moment, she considered the fact that she might be in labor but wrote it off. It had to be another Braxton Hicks contraction. She'd been having them on and off for days.

A second later, the pain subsided, and she crossed the highway, drove a few more miles on the main road, then turned left onto the street leading to Delia's. Last year, Delia had bought a small house outside town near her parents so they could keep the baby while she worked nights. There had been major tension between her and the little boy's father when she refused to live on the reservation.

Another contraction tightened her stomach as she neared the small brick house, and she frowned at the fact that the house looked dark. Only a low light burned in the back bedroom.

Had Delia given up on her and called her parents or a friend to drive them to the hospital? She hadn't said exactly what was wrong with the five-month-old, but what if it was serious?

Anxiety knotted her shoulders as she parked and climbed out. Her back was throbbing, and she paused to catch her breath and let the contraction pass, then shuffled up the stone walkway. Delia's Civic was sitting in the drive, two of the tires flat, confirming that she hadn't been able to drive it.

She stepped up to the door and listened for anyone inside, but silence greeted her. Frowning, she raised her hand and knocked. She continued to massage her back while she waited, but no one answered. Delia must have found a ride....

Still, she turned the knob and the door opened. Her heart pitched, but she inched inside. "Delia?"

She thought she heard a sound from the back. The baby crying?

Alarmed, she hurried toward the bedroom. She glanced in the baby's room, but the baby wasn't in the crib. Then she heard water running. Maybe Delia had the baby in the bathtub and hadn't heard her knock.

Marginally relieved, she called her name again and turned to the left to the woman's bedroom. A lamp burned low beside the bed, and she froze in horror.

Dear God, Delia was lying on the bed, her stomach cut open, blood covering her and the sheets. A scream caught in her throat.

Then she spotted a stone lying at the top of the woman's head and a navel fetish on top of it.

Choking back nausea, she turned to run, but

suddenly something slammed into the back of her head. She cried out, staggering to remain upright and make it outside to her car, but another blow sent her reeling forward.

The world spun, darkness descending as she collapsed on the floor and fell into oblivion.

Chapter Nineteen

Morningside dragged Isabella in front of him, his arm around her throat, his gun poised through the window.

"Listen to me, Morningside," Mason shouted. "You don't want to hurt Isabella. She's the mother of your child."

"But she took my little boy away from me," the man yelled.

"I didn't do that," Isabella cried.

Agent Whitehead's voice echoed over Mason's ear mic. "The back door is locked. We can break in, but I don't want to spook him."

Mason spoke in a low voice into the mic. "No, wait. Let me see if I can convince him to release Isabella."

"Copy that," Agent Whitehead said.

Mason would do his best to get a peaceful resolve, but if Morningside didn't give up, they would take him down. He just didn't want Isabella to be hurt in the process.

"I'm sure Isabella wants you to be part of your son's life," Mason said, intentionally lowering his tone as he inched toward the house. "But if you hurt her, that's not going to happen."

"No, she and her fancy lawyer cut me out of his life, said I was crazy," Morningside yelled. "After all I did for this country, my family doesn't even want me."

"That's not true," Isabella said. "I just want you to get help, to get well."

"Think about it," Mason said as he inched another step closer to the house. "You don't want to hurt the mother of your child."

"Please, Lapu," Isabella pleaded. "Turn yourself in. We'll go for counseling and when you're better, we'll work out a way for you to see Jimmy."

"Do you hear her?" Mason asked. "She wants you to be part of the family. You've had a rough time. Don't make it worse."

"It's already bad," Morningside muttered.

Mason was so close now he could see Isabella trembling in Morningside's hold. "It's not too late for you," he assured the man. "Just think about all the holidays to come. Don't you want to be there for Jimmy on Christmas morning?"

"If I turn myself in, I'll be in jail, not with my little boy on Christmas."

"And if you don't, your son might be left without a mother or father. Is that what you want for him?"

A battle raged in Morningside's eyes. The anguish of what he'd done and what he had become.

"Please, put down the gun, and let Isabella go. Every little boy needs his mommy."

A pain-wrenched sob erupted from Morningside.

Mason held out his hand. "Come on, Morningside, do the right thing for your little boy. Give him the family he deserves."

Morningside looked as if he was going to relent and drop his gun, but a noise sounded from the back, and he pivoted and fired his gun. Isabella screamed and dropped to the floor.

Mason cursed and raced forward, then threw open the door. "Morningside, put down your weapon."

A quick glance told him Isabella was okay. Morningside swung around toward him, his gun raised.

"What was that?" Agent Whitehead said into the mic.

"A noise, then Morningside fired. Where's the sheriff?"

"I'm here," McRae said. "It was just a dog in the trash."

"Relax," Mason said softly to Morningside. "It was just a dog outside. Now put down the gun before someone gets hurt. Because if you shoot me, Morningside, you'll never see your son again."

Of course he was going away for a long time for the bombing and endangering lives, and for murdering three other women, but Mason didn't point that out.

"Please," Isabella said, rising to her knees. "Lapu, I don't want to have to tell our little boy that his father killed a lawman."

Morningside began shaking then, his eyes clouding with emotions, and he started to swing the gun on himself.

Dammit, the son of a bitch wasn't getting off that easy.

Mason jumped him, knocked the gun backward and they fought for it. A shot rang out and hit the ceiling, plaster raining down. Isabella ducked for cover behind the couch, and Agent Whitehead and the sheriff stormed in.

Mason wrestled the gun from Morningside and tossed it to the side, then slammed his fist into Morningside's face. Morningside spit blood, then Mason rolled him to his stomach and slapped the handcuffs on him.

The bastard was going to jail.

CARA STIRRED FROM unconsciousness, her head throbbing. But her back was aching, as well, and her abdomen had seized into a tight knot.

She opened her eyes and tried to look around, but the room was dark, and her vision was blurry. She tried to remember what had happened, panic choking her as she recalled going into Delia's house.

And finding her dead.

Then the world had gone black.

Nausea rolled through her, and she suddenly realized she was moving. She struggled to get up, but hit her head on something hard, and her hands and ankles were bound.

Lord help her. She was in a car, in the trunk. The engine was humming, the heat seeping through the back, the tires grinding over the gravel.

They were on a dirt road.

Good God, Texas had tons of dirt roads that led to open spaces and deserted land.

All places to hide. Or to kill someone and dump their body.

A chill engulfed her as the images of the dead women flashed in her mind. He'd cut out their reproductive organs....

But she was carrying a baby.

Would he hurt her baby just to punish her?

Another pain riddled her belly, and she choked back a panicked sob and tried to think.

Who was driving the car?

Mason was supposed to be on the reservation where Morningside was holding Isabella hostage. So if Isabella's husband was on the res, who had kidnapped her?

Had he escaped and killed Delia then waited to ambush her?

The world blurred again as another pain struck her, and the car hit a pothole, one so deep she bounced and slid sideways, slamming her shoulder into the side of the trunk.

Tears slid down her cheeks, fear robbing her breath.

She wanted to hold her baby in her arms. To love her son and rock him and watch him grow up.

Wrestling with a panic attack, she inhaled sharply. She couldn't fall apart.

Her son depended on her holding it together, so when the driver stopped, she could try to reason with him.

But the image of Delia's brutalized body haunted her, and she was terrified there was no reasoning with the man who'd slaughtered her.

AGENT WHITEHEAD and the sheriff quickly descended, and Sadie joined them to check Isabella for trauma and shock. Carter stood by Sadie's side, a protective male over his new bride.

Mason jerked Morningside up and hauled him toward the sheriff's car.

"You said you were going to help me see my son," Morningside said, although an empty wariness filled his eyes.

A twinge of sympathy surfaced, but Mason couldn't allow emotions. Morningside had been hurt, wronged in the service, but he could have chosen help over the path of destruction he'd sought.

"We'll talk about that once I get your statement," he said. "I want to know details about the bomb you threw into the Winchester Clinic, and all the women you've stalked and murdered."

"What?" Shock stretched across the man's face. "I threw that bomb in the clinic, but everyone got out okay."

"You could have hurt Dr. Winchester and her unborn baby as well as the other patients and the assistant who worked there, a woman with a child that needs her just as much as your son needs his mother."

Morningside's eyes flattened, a faraway look creeping into them as if he was reliving some other time.

"They were the enemy," he said, an odd screech to his voice. "They took my little boy away. We have to destroy the enemy."

"The other patients weren't enemies," Mason barked as he placed his hand on the man's head and shoved him down into the back seat of the car. "And neither was Nellie Thompson, Yolanda Farraday or Angelica Mansfield."

"What the hell are you talking about?" Morningside fought the handcuffs, rattling them as he kicked at the backseat.

"I'm talking about the other women you murdered," Mason barked. "The ones you buried with the stones."

"You've got it all wrong." Morningside balked again, his eyes wild. "I didn't kill those women."

Rage fueled Mason's temper. "You cut out their damn reproductive organs and left navel fetishes at Dr. Winchester's."

Morningside shook his head in denial, then continued to shout his innocence as Mason slammed the door, locking him in the car.

"You did a good job there, Detective Blackpaw," Agent Whitehead said.

"I just want a confession for those murders. I don't want this bastard ever seeing the light of day again."

Agent Whitehead's expression reflected concern. "Something's not right."

Mason turned his back to the man who was ranting and beating at the window. "Don't tell me you believe him."

She worried her bottom lip with her teeth. "He's definitely disturbed, and I heard him confess to the bombing, but I've been thinking about this. It's unusual for a serial killer to change his M.O. Morningside chose a public venue to make a statement with the bomb. That's a totally different profile from a man who literally butchers a woman in cold blood and buries her in a ritualistic style."

Mason glanced at the car where Morningside was still vehemently denying the murder accusations, and cold fear knotted his insides. They'd found all those photos on his wall, which made him look guilty.

And he'd been ready to beat the hell out of the man for a confession.

But what if he was wrong?

Sweat exploded on his forehead, and he gestured

to the sheriff. "Drive him to the station and lock him up. I have to call Cara and make sure she's okay."

Agent Whitehead stepped aside, and he punched in Cara's number. Her voice mail clicked on automatically, which struck him as odd. Dammit, where was she?

Frantic, he called Brody. "She's not here, man. She left a note saying she was making a house call."

"How long ago was that?"

"Couple of hours," Brody said. "Why? Is something wrong?"

Mason explained that they'd arrested Morningside, but that there might be a second suspect, that the Navel Fetish Killer might still be on the loose.

"I'll ride out and check her cabin," Brody said.

"Let me know if she's there." Mason paced by his car while the sheriff climbed in the front of the squad car and started the engine. But Agent Whitehead still looked worried.

His mind raced with the possibilities. The clinic was closed, and Sadie Whitefeather was here. Maybe Sherese would know.

He called her number, his heart ticking as he waited on the reply. Four rings later and Sherese answered.

"Sherese, it's Detective Blackpaw. Do you know where Cara is?"

"One of our patients, Delia Nez, called in that her little boy was sick and she had car trouble and couldn't make it to the clinic. Dr. Winchester drove out to see them."

Mason pinched the bridge of his nose. "Have you heard from her since?"

"No." Sherese's voice cracked. "Why? Is something wrong?"

"I don't know," Mason said. "Give me that address."

Sherese recited it, and he put it to memory and raced toward his car.

Agent Whitehead followed on his tail. "What's going on?"

"I don't know. Cara took a house call. I'm going to see if she's all right."

"Do you want me to go with you?"

"No, go with the sheriff and see what you can get out of Morningside. If he killed those women, find out."

She nodded and headed to the squad car. Isabella and Sadie and Carter were watching. "Stay here with the women," he told Carter. "Make sure they're safe."

Carter pulled Sadie to him, and she hugged Isabella to her side, and the three of them walked into the house while he tore down the drive from the Morningsides' house.

The place was on the other side of town, a good ten miles away. He rolled down the window, struggling to breathe, the images of the dead women's corpses in the ground taunting him with each mile.

He couldn't allow that to happen to Cara.

Not to the woman he loved.

But what if you're too late?

Tremors racked his body, and his arms were jerking so badly he almost had to pull over. He cursed his weakness.

He could not fall apart now.

Hopefully Cara and the baby were safe. Cara was simply doing her usual thing, taking care of others. She had to be alive.

Surely God wouldn't allow something bad to happen to a wonderful, giving woman like her.

He crossed through town, weaving through traffic, and using his siren to bypass the worst, then maneuvered the side streets until he reached Delia Nez's place.

He swiped perspiration from his forehead as he spotted Cara's Pathfinder and parked behind it. But anxiety clawed at him as he approached the house.

Except for a dim light burning in a back room, the house was dark.

Not a good sign.

He pulled his gun, inching up the steps and keeping his senses honed for sounds inside. Voices. A cry. A child.

Anything.

But it was eerily quiet.

Pulse pounding, he pushed open the front screen door and crept inside. The den was dark but appeared empty.

The light was coming from a back room. Walking as quietly as he could, he crept toward the room. To the left, he spotted a nursery. Empty, as well.

But an acrid odor seeped from the other room, an odor that he'd smelled too much of lately.

The stench of death.

Praying it wasn't Cara, he held his gun at the ready in case he was walking into an ambush, then scanned the room. He'd seen a lot of dead people in his career, and the women he'd seen buried lately had been among the worst.

But this woman hadn't been buried yet. Instead, the bastard had butchered her and left her in a pool of her own blood with an amulet resting on a stone at her head.

Bile rose to his throat. Morningside wasn't the Navel Fetish killer.

No, some other man was.

And he'd used Delia Nez to lure Cara into his trap.

Chapter Twenty

Fear immobilized Mason for a heartbeat, but his training kicked in. God help him, he didn't have time to hesitate.

Every second Cara was missing meant she might be closer to her death.

He punched Agent Whitehead's number, quickly scanning the room for any signs of Cara. Her medical bag sat on the floor, yet it remained unopened.

Meaning the woman had been dead when she'd arrived, and Cara had been ambushed.

Cold sweat beaded his skin, and he growled at the phone, relieved when Agent Whitehead finally answered.

"It's Blackpaw. Did you get anything from Morningside?"

"Nothing new. He's in a holding cell now. He still insists he didn't murder those women."

"Dammit, I don't think he did, either. Cara was supposed to be on a call, but I'm at the woman's house and she's dead. Same M.O. as the others."

"Dr. Winchester is there?"

"No, she's missing," Mason said through clenched teeth. "The real Navel Fetish Killer has her."

The agent's breath whooshed out. "What can I do?"

"Send a crime unit over here. And see if your people can trace Cara's phone. Her medical bag is here, but she keeps her phone on her." The phone was a long shot, but it was the only place he knew to start. Hopefully the killer hadn't found it and tossed it.

Mason gave her the coordinates, then yanked on a pair of latex gloves and pressed two fingers to the woman's body. Rigor had already set in.

The killer had probably watched her bleed out when he'd made the phony call to Cara's answering service.

A photograph of a small baby sat on the woman's nightstand, and another bolt of fear slammed into him. So far, the Navel Fetish Killer hadn't hurt any children. He prayed he hadn't started with this woman's baby.

But where was the child?

Heart banging against his chest, he rushed into the bathroom and checked the tub and closet, but they were empty. Relieved, he combed the rest of the house, the baby's room and closet, the pantry. A sickening thought occurred to him, stories of other cases where people had murdered children and thrown them away, and he made himself check the trashcans outside.

When he found them empty, he leaned forward, braced his hands on his knees and drew a relieved breath.

Still, where was the child? Had the killer taken it with him?

CARA BATTLED PANIC as the car rolled to an abrupt stop, jarring her so badly pain rocked through her abdomen again, fear choking her.

What if this was the real thing? Not another Braxton Hicks contraction?

Dear God, she couldn't be going into labor now.

Tears welled in her eyes, but she blinked them back. She had to be strong. Had to figure out a way to escape, to reach Mason.

Remembering her phone at her waist, she struggled to reach it, but her hands were bound behind her back. She raised her knees, trying to bring them high enough for her to somehow get to it, but her belly was too big.

She fumbled, twisting and turning, desperate to untie her hands, but suddenly the trunk lid swung up. It had been so dark in the trunk that for a moment light blinded her, and she had to blink to adjust her eyes.

The sign for the old fishing lodge at Devil's Creek swayed unsteadily in the wind, making another knot of fear clamp her throat. The place was miles from nowhere.

No one would see their car or hear them out here.

Then a cold hand grabbed her arm and wrenched her upward. "Come on, Doc, it's time we settle this."

Cara's throat closed at the sound of the deep voice. A familiar voice.

My God, no wonder he'd known her patients and their history.

She wrestled with his grip as he hauled her from the trunk. "Why?" she whispered. "Why are you doing this?"

But he didn't answer. His eyes blazed a cold trail over her, then he dragged her through the woods.

Cara screamed for help, but they were in the middle of nowhere, and she knew no one could hear her.

He was going to kill her and bury her here with the stones.

Then what would happen to her baby?

Mason met Agent Whitehead and the crime unit at the door. Jody's face was familiar as well as the young guy with her.

"I was hoping we wouldn't have to process another one," Jody said.

"So was I," Mason said grimly.

He turned to Agent Whitehead while Jody and the crime tech began to examine the body. "Any word on Cara's phone?"

"Not yet."

"Listen," Mason said. "The victim had a baby. The child is not here, so we need to find him."

Agent Whitehead's face paled. "You think he took the baby?"

"I don't know. I'm going to look through her phone to see if I can find a relative."

Agent Whitehead nodded. "I'll have one of my guys see what he can find."

Mason searched Delia Nez's purse and found her cell phone, then scrolled through her calls. He found a listing for a Polly and Larry Nez so he hit connect. The phone rang several times and rolled to voice mail, so he left a message saying they needed to contact him immediately, that it was regarding their daughter.

"My guys are searching for an address for the parents," Agent Whitehead said. She took a look at the body, then pivoted, worrying her bottom lip with her teeth again.

"We're missing something. Except for the bombing, Morningside fit the profile."

"There has to be someone else who fits it, as well." Mason paced to the front room then out the door. Storm clouds rolled across the sky, the sun waning. It would be night soon, and he was no closer to finding Cara and his baby or this killer.

Mentally he ticked over the details of the profile, over the killer's M.O., over his conversation with Cara. Agent Whitehead stepped outside but remained silent for a moment.

"We missed something," she said again. "I keep thinking about the overkill with the women."

Mason raked a hand through his hair. "Cara was disturbed at the way the organs were removed." He snapped his fingers. "What if our killer had some kind of medical training?"

Agent Whitehead's eyes widened. "You may be on to something. The other characteristics of the profile could be the same, but if he had medical training, that would narrow down our list." She clenched her cell phone. "Let me call our analyst and have her search military records."

He gripped the porch rail as he listened to her talk to her associate. "Just like before, we think he's a Native American, probably suffering PTSD, was in the military. He may have lost his family while he was deployed, the wife left him, or had a child and gave it up for adoption. Narrow it down to men with medical training, as well." A pause. "Yes, call me back when you have something."

"I'll call Cara's assistant," Mason said. "She knew the patients. Maybe one of their spouses or ex-boyfriends fits that description."

When she answered, she sounded frantic. "Did you find Cara?"

"No," Mason said. "But Delia was murdered and Cara's missing."

A terrified sob wrenched Sherese's throat. "You think he has Cara?"

Mason had to swallow twice to make his voice work. "Yes, and Morningside is in custody so he didn't kill Delia. The killer fits the same profile as Morningside except he had medical training. Can you think of anyone associated with the clinic, maybe a patient's spouse or ex who fits that description?"

"I don't know about the background of all the patients," she said, her voice breaking. "I'd have to look at their files and they were destroyed in the fire."

Dammit. If he had Cara's computer he could send it to her. Maybe it was in her car. He rushed outside to retrieve it but it wasn't inside. "If you think of anyone call me back."

"I will, and Mason, please bring Cara back."

"I intend to." Although defeat and fear weighed on him. He had no idea how long the killer had held the other victims before he'd killed them. And if he was playing out his end game, his violence and timing might be escalating.

His cell phone beeped that he had another call. It was the Nezes, so he quickly connected it. A moment later, the head medical examiner arrived, and Mason gestured for him to go inside.

"Detective Blackpaw," a male voice said into the phone. "This is Larry Nez. You called about my daughter?"

Mason hated this part of the job. "Sir, first can you tell me where your grandson is?"

"He's with us," the man said, an edge to his voice. "Why? Where's our daughter?"

"I'm sorry, Mr. Nez, I hate to tell you this, but she's dead. I'm at her house now."

"We'll be right there."

"No—" But before he could respond, the man hung up on him.

Agent Whitehead was on the phone again, her body tense as she scribbled something on a notepad. "Thanks."

"Larry Nez is on his way over," he told the agent.

Worry creased Agent Whitehead's forehead. "I have a couple of names who fit the profile. A man named Les Williams, his mother was part Comanche and he grew up on a res outside Houston. He had some medical training in the military and was released because he lost his hand and could no longer perform surgery."

So the man had his reasons for being bitter. "Where is he now?"

"He's been suffering from depression and alcohol abuse. The last address I have is a rehab center not too far from town."

"How about the other man?"

"Farr Nacona, he was trained as a paramedic and was discharged from the military because of an injury. He applied to med school but was denied because of emotional problems stemming from his stint in the service. Last address for him is near the river."

He frowned, searching his memory banks. Where had he heard that name before? On the reservation?

"I'll check out Williams," Agent Whitehead said. "You take Nacona."

Mason nodded. "All right. Let me know if anything comes in on Cara's phone."

A second later, a car pulled up and screeched to a stop. A man in his mid-fifties jumped out, his face frantic with worry. "Where's my daughter?"

Mason blocked him from entering the house, and Agent Whitehead gently took his arm. "Mr. Nez?"

The man tried to wrench away. "Where is she? I have to see her."

"I'm so sorry for your loss," Agent Whitehead said. "But you don't want to go in there."

"Yes, I do," he cried. "I have to see my little girl."

"Not like that you don't," Mason said gruffly. "Trust me, you want to remember your daughter smiling at you, not the way she is now."

"The medical examiner is with her," Agent Whitehead said. "He'll take care of her and transport her to the morgue for an autopsy."

The man broke down into tears. "What…what did he do to her?" Shock and horror filled his eyes as he looked up at Mason. "Don't tell me this is that monster who killed those other women."

Mason exchanged a frustrated look with the agent. "We're not certain," Agent Whitehead said, hedging. "But we have a strong lead as to who did it, and we're going to make an arrest soon."

"You should have already done that!" the man bellowed. "If you had, my daughter would still be alive."

Guilt suffused Mason. Yes, they should have.

And because they hadn't, Cara might die, too.

The medical examiner must have overheard them because he stepped outside. He was a kind, older fellow with white hair and wire-rimmed glasses.

"Please, Mr. Nez, go home and take care of your wife and grandchild," he said. "And let these officers find out who did this."

The man collapsed onto the steps, and buried his head in his arms, his body shaking with grief. The medical examiner sank down beside him to comfort him, and gestured for Mason and Agent White-head to leave.

"I promise you we'll find him," Mason said to Nez. "I won't stop until I do."

The man didn't acknowledge him, and he didn't expect him to. He had just lost his daughter.

Agent Whitehead jogged to her car, and he sprinted to his, calling Sherese as he ripped from the parking lot. "Sherese, do you recall a man named Farr Nacona? Was he related to one of your patients?"

"Oh, my God, you don't think he's the Navel Fetish Killer?"

"It's possible. Why? Do you know him?"

"Yes, but he's not related to a patient. Cara felt sorry for him because he was hurt in Afghanistan and gave him a job."

Mason's chest clenched. "What kind of job?"

"As a janitor at the clinic."

Mason cursed. The man had been right under

their noses all along. And he'd used the job Cara had given him at the clinic to gather his list of victims.

And to stalk Cara so he would know her every movement.

"PLEASE DON'T DO THIS, Farr," Cara cried.

He had unbound her feet so she could walk, and he pushed her farther into the woods. Trees rose above her, shading any light, the darkness surrounding her so disorienting that she had no idea where they were or where they were going.

"Shut up," he hissed.

Ahead, Cara saw the faint outline of the old fishing lodge and breathed a small sigh of relief. Maybe he didn't plan to kill her right away. Maybe he'd keep her alive long enough for Mason to find her.

But how would he do that? They had all been convinced that Morningside was the killer. Once Mason saved Isabella, she thought they'd be safe.

Mason might not even know she was missing.

A tree limb scraped her arm, and she clenched her teeth, ducking to avoid another low branch. Her back was throbbing, and another contraction tightened her belly. She winced in pain, pushing forward as Farr shoved her into the clearing, then half dragged her up the steps to the old lodge.

"Please, Farr," Cara begged. "I need help. I'm in labor."

He cursed, shoved open the door and pushed her inside.

"Why are you doing this?" she asked, her voice weak as she breathed through the pain. "I tried to help you. I gave you a job."

"You made me a janitor," he said, his dark eyes blazing with a kind of rage Cara had never seen before. "I was a war hero, a medic, and after all I did, you and the others didn't respect me. You made me clean your floors."

"But I didn't know," Cara said.

"Then I watched you tell all those women to give up their babies. Our people believe women are supposed to be kind and loving and nurturing, yet you tell them to throw their children away. That family does not matter anymore."

"That's not true," Cara cried, but another spasm cut off her protest.

"Please help me," she whispered. "I need to go to the hospital."

Farr released a bitter laugh. "You weren't listening, were you, Dr. Winchester? I will deliver your baby, then you will pay for your sins."

Chapter Twenty-One

Mason flew toward Nacona's house, praying the man had taken Cara there. If not, he didn't have a clue as to where to look.

His cell phone jangled and he quickly connected the call.

"Detective Blackpaw, I'm at the rehab facility where Williams has been," Agent Whitehead said. "He has an alibi for all the murders. The woman who runs the halfway house confirmed he hasn't left the premises for two weeks."

"Nacona is our man," Mason said. "Sherese, Cara's assistant, said he worked as a janitor at the Winchester Clinic and at the clinic on the reservation, as well."

"That fits," Agent Whitehead said. "After receiving service awards and having medical training of his own, that job must have been demeaning to him."

"I'm on my way to the address I have for him now. Ask your people to see what they can dig up on him. Maybe he has family or some property where he might take Cara."

"I'm on it."

"Anything on the phone yet?"

"Not yet, but I'll check on it right now."

He thanked her and hung up, then called his partner, Miles McGregor. He'd taken off a few days to be with his new wife Jordan, but he needed him now.

"McGregor," Mason said without preamble. "Dr. Winchester has been kidnapped by the Navel Fetish Killer."

Miles muttered an obscenity. "What can I do?"

"We believe the man's name is Farr Nacona. He worked as a janitor for Cara. I'm on my way to his house to look for them, but since the first body was found on the BBL, it occurred to me that he might bring her back there."

"I'll call Brody and get his security teams to comb the property."

"Thanks. I'll alert the tribal police on the reservation."

They disconnected, and he dialed Liam Runninghorse as he swerved onto the old dirt road. The hogan where Nacona lived was on the far end of the reservation in a deserted area that offered privacy.

And far enough from neighbors so no one could hear a woman's cries for help.

The phone finally clicked as Runninghorse answered, and he quickly explained the situation. "Call Sadie and Carter and alert them. I'm almost to Nacona's place now."

"Do you want me to meet you?"

"Let me see if he's there first. Meanwhile, you and the chief check other places on the res. Look for any deserted hogans and ask around. Maybe someone on the res knows where he might go."

"Good idea. I'll let you know if we turn up anything." Liam paused. "And call if you need backup, Blackpaw."

"I will." Although if the bastard had hurt his son or harmed one hair on Cara's head, he'd kill him with his bare hands.

He hung up, then pressed the accelerator and raced past shrub brush, barren soil, mesquites and a row of vacant hogans that were in disrepair. Suspicion nagged at him, and he slowed, looking for a car but didn't see one anywhere in sight. Still, he scanned the bushes beyond in case he'd stowed it behind some trees, but nothing stuck out.

Deciding they were clear, he pushed the gas again and bounced over the ruts in the road, his teeth clenched as he spotted the cabin at the edge of the woods.

He didn't see a car there, either.

Hell, the man could have ditched it, or maybe he knew a side road and left it there then walked in on foot to throw him off.

Gun at the ready, he climbed from his car and strode toward the wooden framed structure that looked as if it was rotting on its frame. An old tire rim lay to the side along with some gardening tools, the yard was overgrown, and two windowpanes were broken out.

Not a comforting sight.

He inched closer, ears cocked for sounds of Cara or Nacona, but the sound of the wind rocking an old porch swing screeched eerily like a ghost pushing it back and forth.

Gravel crunched beneath his boots as he slipped up to the window and peeked inside. Dusty furniture covered with old blankets filled the front room, liquor bottles were piled on the kitchen counter, and the bed was unmade.

He sucked in a sharp breath, his instincts telling him the place was empty, but still he had to be sure. So he crept around back and pushed at the door. Unlocked.

Nothing to steal in the place anyway.

He slowly entered, senses honed, but a quick sweep of the bathroom, then the bedroom and den, and defeat settled in.

The house was empty.

Where in the hell was Cara?

CARA SHUDDERED AS ANOTHER pain ripped through her, then she felt a gush of warmth on her thighs. She didn't have to look down to know her water had broken. Nacona had shoved her into a chair and stood back and watched as she suffered one contraction after another.

"My water broke," she said, lifting her chin with

a defiant tilt. "Please let me go to the bathroom and clean up."

He folded his arms and studied her for a moment, then walked over to a duffel bag, removed a hospital gown and pair of scrub pants and flung them at her. "All right, but make it quick."

So he had come prepared.

The very idea that he'd planned this made bile rise to her throat.

He jerked her toward the bathroom. Cara cringed at his touch, the memory of what he'd done to those other women buried deep in her soul.

"You'll have to untie me," she said when he stopped at the bathroom door.

His gaze met hers, an emptiness in the depths that terrified her more than words. "You can't escape, so don't even try."

He didn't have to tell her that. For heaven's sake, she was in the throes of labor, and too exhausted to run. Slowly he untied her, and she rubbed at her sore wrists, then she slipped into the bathroom and shut the door.

Grateful for a moment of privacy, she shrugged off her maternity pants, glad to get rid of the soiled clothes. Thankfully her maternity shirt had covered her phone so he hadn't taken it from her. Knowing this might be her only chance, she called Mason's number, but she heard Farr at the door and hid it back in the soaked pants then pushed it into the corner of the floor. Her shirt came next but she left on her bra, then dragged on the scrubs and tied them loosely at the waist.

Another pain seized her, and she leaned over the sink and breathed through it. When she glanced at the mirror, she hardly recognized herself. Her hair was wildly disheveled and sweat-soaked, dirt from the trunk of the car streaked her face, and her eyes were red and puffy from holding back the tears she desperately wanted to cry.

But she refused to give him the pleasure of showing her fear.

She splashed cold water on her face, then noticed a dry cloth hanging on the towel rack, doused it in cold water and pressed it to the back of her neck.

Suddenly the door swung open, and his gaze scorched her with contempt. Grasping for control, she ignored him, rinsed her face again, then clutched the washcloth in her hand as he yanked her from the bathroom and shoved her toward the metal bed in the corner.

Tears threatened but she blinked them back. She might have her baby here, but she would not die today.

Somehow she'd find a way to save herself and her son.

DESPAIR THREATENED TO knock Mason to his knees. His phone buzzed and he snatched it up, relieved to see Cara's number. He answered immediately. "Hello, Cara, are you all right?" But no one was on the line. Still, hope budded. If she'd tried to call him, she was still alive.

He put the call on hold, then called Julie and told her to have the call traced. "I'll get back you ASAP," Julie said.

He hung up, his chest tight. Cara wasn't in Nacona's house. So where the hell had he taken her?

God, please don't let me be too late.

Knowing he didn't have time to fall apart, he forced himself through the house, looking for clues as to where the man might have gone.

He checked the kitchen drawers, the cabinets, the desk, then looked inside the closet for clues about the man.

His blood ran cold at what he found. Pictures of each of the victims' burial spots had been tacked inside the door. Remembering that he took a souvenir of their hair, he checked the shoebox inside and an old cigar box but found nothing. He hunted for the buffalo skinner knife but it wasn't there, either.

Because he had it with him to use on Cara.

The realization made his head roll.

Remembering he'd woven the hair into the navel fetish pouches, he scanned the wall. His gaze fell on the bow above the man's bed, suspicions kicking in, and he crossed the room to it, his heart stuttering at the sight of the different colored strands.

One from each of the murder victims.

Dammit. Cara's hair would not go in there.

His cell phone jangled, a sharp sound that jarred

him from the disturbing evidence that confirmed in his mind that Nacona was their man.

Agent Whitehead's name flashed on the caller ID, and Mason stabbed the button to connect. "Please tell me you have something."

"We've tracked the car to a deserted road near Devil's Creek."

Adrenaline surged through Mason. "I know where that is. I'm heading to my car. Text me the coordinates."

"They're coming to you now. I'll try to meet you there, but it may take me a while. There was an accident up ahead, and traffic is at a complete standstill."

Mason ran to his car, explaining about the bow as he started down the drive.

"I'll call McRae and have him send the crime unit there. When we catch this creep, he needs to fry," she said.

Mason mumbled agreement, then pushed the gas to the limits. Devil's Creek was only a few miles away, but very much off the beaten path.

The fact that Nacona had taken Cara there reminded him of the words he'd written in blood and left on her pillow, and made his heart harden.

He barreled down the road, spitting gravel and dust, half on, half off the mangled road as he followed the GPS. A quick turn to the right, another dirt road, a sign for the old fishing lodge that used to cater to hunters and fishermen who wanted an escape.

It had been shut down long ago although he'd heard talk that one of the Natives was thinking of restoring it.

He wove along the narrow road, his lights shining across the desolate terrain, the occasional sound of a night creature echoing in the night. Seconds stretched into precious minutes that made him so anxious nausea swirled through him.

He had to make it to Cara in time.

He couldn't lose her or his son tonight.

THE CONTRACTIONS WERE coming one on top of the other. Cara barely had time in between them to catch her breath.

"Please, take me to the hospital," she said. "I've delivered enough babies to know that anything can go wrong."

Farr made a tsking sound. "There you go again, not trusting me." He jerked her arm, pulling her up from the chair. "You're going to have this baby the natural way, just as God intended."

"Where are you taking me?" she asked as he dragged her toward the door.

"You'll see. Your baby is part of our people. He will be brought into this world as he should be."

Cara gritted her teeth as another pain struck her. But Nacona had no sympathy. He pushed her outside and hauled her through the woods. She doubled over, breathing through the agony, and searched the darkness as he forced her into the woods.

If Mason didn't find her before she delivered the baby, what did Farr intend to do? Kill her and take her child?

MASON FLEW OVER THE graveled road, hands sweating as he gripped the steering wheel to keep the car on the road. Dirt and gravel spewed behind him, but storm clouds rolled across the sky, the sound of thunder bursting into the night.

He prayed the rain held off. A downpour would slow him down, and every minute counted.

Swinging the vehicle to the right, he wove down the tree-snarled road, racing past woods and casting his eyes around in case Nacona had set up a watch somewhere. Five miles deep into the thicket, the old dilapidated fishing lodge came into view.

He spotted an old beat-up car to the side, and relief warred with fear. They had to be here.

He just prayed he wasn't too late.

Pulling his gun from his holster, he parked and climbed out, scanning the perimeter. If Nacona was inside the lodge and had heard the car, he'd be waiting.

His weapon was a knife. But that didn't mean he didn't have a gun, as well. Only that he preferred to use the knife on his victims.

At first glance, everything seemed quiet. So quiet that his heart began to race. If he wasn't inside, where the hell had he taken Cara?

Breath stalled in his chest as he crept forward. He

inched up to the side window and glanced inside, but the room was dark. The building was a one-story structure with rooms on each side of a center welcoming area. He peeked inside each window as he went, but it appeared empty.

The creek gurgled behind the lodge, and he slipped through the back door, frowning at the sight of the decay and dirt in the abandoned rooms. Something creaked, and he hesitated to listen, then crept toward the noise.

A side room off the main lobby had been an office at one point, but there was a cot in there and a bathroom was attached.

He poked his head in, but no one was there.

But Cara's soiled clothes were piled in the corner of the bathroom.

A choked sound caught in his throat. What had Nacona done to her?

Chapter Twenty-Two

Anger mingled with rage as Mason searched each room of the lodge. But the room where he'd found Cara's discarded clothing was the only one with any sign that they'd been there.

Adrenaline fueling him, he forced himself to think like a detective, not a man who might have just lost the two most precious people in the world to him.

Falling back on his tracking skills, he spotted footprints leading out the door. Scuffmarks also darkened the wood flooring, an indication that someone had been dragged. Emotions thickened his throat as he imagined the scenario, but he quickly blocked them out.

He followed the prints outside, noted that they led to the right along the water through the woods. Using every tracking skill he possessed, he followed them, searching for a broken twig, leaves crunched beneath the weight of the footprints.

A torn piece of clothing. Blue.

Like the scrub suits he'd seen at Cara's clinic.

The man's footprints continued, Cara's oddly varying in depth, then an occasional spot where it looked as if she might have fallen to her knees.

Was she hurt?

He flashed back to the soaked clothing, and his gut tightened. She was in labor.

Dear God…

A second later, he pulled himself back together and forged on. A few more feet and he heard voices.

Then a gut-wrenching scream of pain.

It tore at his heart, but at least Cara was still alive.

Determination heated his blood, and he ran toward the direction of the sound. He pushed aside brush and weeds, flying over rocks and broken limbs from a storm, the sound of thunder mingling with the harshness of his own breath.

Another scream, and he realized he was close. He jogged toward the sound, then halted when he spotted a teepee set up next to the river.

Cara was on her hands and knees, writhing in pain. "Please, the baby is coming."

Nacona stood above her like some ancient warfighting Indian, the buffalo skinner knife glinting in the dark. "Crawl in the teepee and we'll deliver the child," Nacona barked.

"Please don't hurt my baby," Cara pleaded.

Mason's lungs volleyed for air. He couldn't startle Nacona, or he might drive the knife into Cara and kill her and the baby.

Padding as quietly as he could, just as he'd been taught on the reservation, he crept through the brush, anguish searing him when Cara released another cry.

"The baby's crowning," she said through a labored breath. "Please, promise me you won't hurt my son."

"Don't worry. I will raise him as my own."

Nacona was so caught up in his evil, twisted plan that he didn't hear him approach.

Mason raised his gun and aimed, but suddenly Nacona pivoted toward him. Holding the knife above Cara's head, he shoved her into the teepee on her hands and knees.

Fury emboldened Mason, and he circled back to the other side to throw off Nacona. Cara cried out, then Nacona turned and scanned the woods as if he sensed he was there.

Mason lunged forward and jumped him, throwing his weight into the man. Nacona bellowed out in their Native language, and Mason knocked the knife from his hand. It skittered into the dirt a few feet away, and Nacona punched him and crawled toward it.

But Mason pressed the barrel of his gun to Nacona's temple. "Move and I'll shoot you, you bastard."

Nacona looked up at him from the ground and spit. "You are a disservice to our people. My father was a staunch Comanche. He taught me to hunt and kill when I was a boy."

"He taught you to kill women?" Mason growled.

"He taught me that Comanches looked upon their children as their most precious gift. They were supposed to be protective of their young and rarely punished them." He spewed venom from his eyes. "The girls were taught to sew and cook and take care of their babies."

"Dr. Winchester helps women do that," Mason snapped.

"No, she encourages them to throw children away. When I went on my vision quest at fifteen, I saw my future. I was meant to rid the world of mothers who did not follow the ways."

"How dare you use our culture to condone what you did," Mason said. "You're nothing but a common murderer."

His eyes blazed with hate and a sickness that had obviously stolen his mind. "I was honoring our traditions. The mother—"

"Is supposed to be revered for giving birth and taking care of the family," Mason said. "Not butchered like an animal."

Cara cried out again, and his heart pounded. The baby was coming.

Nacona took that second to try to escape and shoved Mason. They rolled into the dirt, exchanging blow after blow. Nacona fought like a wild animal, kicking Mason in the gut and crawling toward the river.

But Mason caught him and they fought again. Nacona slugged him in the face; blood trickled down

Mason's nose. But the sound of Cara's crying fueled his rage and adrenaline kicked in.

He flipped Nacona onto his back, then slammed the butt of the gun against his head so hard the man's eyes rolled back in his head.

Teeth clenched, he hurriedly searched to make sure he didn't have another weapon on him, then removed the handcuffs inside his jacket, dragged the man toward a tree and handcuffed him to one of the large sturdy branches.

A sound of pain ripped through the air, Cara's scream, and he raced to the teepee to her.

CARA REMINDED HERSELF to breathe, that other women had delivered their babies alone and survived.

But another contraction told her it was time to push, and tears spilled from her eyes. What if something went wrong? What if Nacona took her little boy and hurt him?

What if he killed her, and she never got the chance to hold him and love him and raise him?

Suddenly the flap door of the teepee moved, and she swallowed hard to keep from screaming at the man who'd kidnapped her. "Please, don't hurt my son."

"I won't." The sound of the man's voice jarred her, and she looked up and saw Mason's face poking through the doorway.

"Mason," she whispered.

He fell to his knees in front of her. "I'm here, Cara, it's going to be all right."

"But Nacona—"

"He's alive and handcuffed to a tree," Mason said, although his dark tone indicated he would just as soon have killed the man.

Cara nodded, but there wasn't time to say more. She felt as if she was ripping in two. "He's coming now," she said, her voice laced with panic.

"Just tell me what to do," Mason said calmly.

His reassuring tone and soothing hand on hers sent a wave of emotion through her. "I can't believe you're here."

"I can't believe we're having a baby," he said with a twitch of a smile.

The pain intensified. "Help me get these pants off," she said.

Mason nodded and worked quickly to remove the garment, then she hiked her knees up. "I have to push. Can you find something clean to put under me for the baby?"

He nodded, removed his jacket then noticed a duffel bag inside the teepee.

"It's his," Cara said. "He might have supplies."

Cold rage swept through Mason. The SOB had been prepared to watch Cara deliver, then what would he have done?

"Mason, hurry," Cara whispered.

He shook himself out of the moment, raced over to the bag. Just as she'd predicted, there were towels inside, along with a baby blanket and surgical scissors.

He brought them all to Cara, then laid towels beneath her. She gripped her knees and began to push.

"I see his head," Mason shouted.

"Good." Cara relaxed for a moment, then braced herself again and pushed once more. Pain rocked her body, but excitement made her bear down and push again.

"His head is out," Mason said.

"When you see his shoulders, gently take them and help him," Cara instructed.

Mason nodded, his gaze meeting hers. Love for him overwhelmed her at the depth of feeling in his expressive eyes.

She had to get their baby here.

She bore down, gritted her teeth and gave it her best effort. Suddenly she felt her son slip from her body.

"I have him!" Mason shouted. "He's here."

Cara listened for a cry, and panicked when she didn't hear it. "Turn him over and massage his chest," she said. "Make sure he's breathing."

For a moment fear darkened Mason's eyes, but he did as she said, and a second later, the sound of her baby's cry rang out.

It was the most beautiful sound she'd ever heard.

Then Mason wiped off the baby, wrapped him in the blanket and placed him in her arms.

Cara kissed her son on the forehead, tears of joy blurring her eyes as Mason moved up beside her.

"I'm going to name him Maska," Cara said as she looked up at him. "It means that he's strong."

Mason tucked a strand of hair behind her ear, touched that she'd chosen a Native American name. "Strong like his mama." Then he pressed a kiss to the baby's head and cradled them both in his arms.

Cara curled up against him, grateful they had all survived.

MASON WAS SO MOVED by the sight of his baby in Cara's arms that he couldn't speak. He wanted to promise her that he'd love her and his son and take care of them forever.

But reality interceded when he heard Nacona chanting in their Native language. "I'm going to call an ambulance and the sheriff," Mason said.

Cara caught his arm as if she didn't want him to leave. But he had to.

Nacona had to be arrested and she needed an ambulance.

She nestled the baby to her breast and Mason swallowed, the image moving something inside him that he'd never felt before. An unbelievably strong bond and protective instinct that would never die.

Memorizing the moment in his mind, he stepped outside, and made the call.

But anxiety tugged at him as he waited on the

ambulance and sheriff. He and Cara still hadn't discussed their situation.

In fact, he had no idea where his place would be in her life or his son's.

He only knew that he wanted to be with them.

But how could he be a family man and do his job?

Even if he figured out a way to make it work, could Cara forgive him for not believing in them in the first place?

CARA HAD NEVER FELT so emotional in her life. Between the terrifying ordeal with Nacona, her hormones, and finally holding her little son in her arms, tears flooded her eyes. Her little boy was perfect, not just ten fingers and ten toes, but he had the dark coloring, high cheekbones and black hair of his father.

She wanted him to grow up to be just like him.

The wail of a siren rent the night, then the ambulance arrived.

Disappointment ballooned in Cara's chest when Mason chose to oversee Nacona's arrest instead of riding with her to the hospital.

Was he pulling away already? Trying to remind her that his work would always come before her and their son?

Chapter Twenty-Three

It took forever for the sheriff to arrive and for them to transport Nacona. The sick man had lapsed into a sullen silence, content in his twisted logic that what he'd done was warranted by his vision quest.

Mason wanted him out of his sight. Every time he thought about the fact that he'd almost killed Cara, he wanted to rip out his throat with his bare hands.

By the time he arrived at the hospital, Cara and the baby were settled into a room. He cracked the door open a notch and peeked inside, but Cara was sleeping and so was the baby. He watched them for several minutes, soaking in the sight of her and his son.

But the fact that they hadn't discussed his relationship—or *their* relationship—made him hesitate to go inside.

Cara and the baby were a family. But where did he fit in their lives?

Maybe they would be better without him. His work would only bring danger and uncertainty to them.

Yet the fact that his own father had abandoned

him haunted him. How could he allow his son to grow up and think that he hadn't wanted him?

EARLY THE NEXT MORNING, Cara woke to the sound of her baby crying. A smile softened her mouth as she reached for her little boy and put him to her breast. He latched on immediately, and she stroked his soft dark hair, amazed that he was actually in her arms.

She had never felt such happiness and love.

Yet a sliver of sadness dampened her joy. She wanted Mason to be with her. For them to be a family.

But he hadn't shown up the night before, and he wasn't here this morning.

She understood his job and his need the night before to make sure Nacona was locked away.

But that had been hours ago, and he hadn't even called. Had he decided he didn't want a ready-made family?

That he didn't love her?

She traced a finger over her baby's cheek and blinked back tears. "I love you, little Maska."

And if Mason didn't want them, her love would have to be enough.

MASON STUDIED THE faces of the boys around the camp, grateful they had enjoyed the lesson he'd taught them that morning. For a group of rambunctious preadolescents, they'd eagerly listened to his take on tracking and had enjoyed the hike through the deserted terrain where he'd had them practice skills.

But as they disbanded, he thought of his own son. Just a tiny baby now, but he needed guidance.

A man's guidance.

His *father's* guidance.

Dammit, what was wrong with him? Why was he here volunteering to help other people's kids when he should be with his own today?

Cara's beautiful, strong, brave face flashed in his mind. She had faced down a sadistic killer and given birth to his son, and what had he done?

Abandoned her again like a coward?

And why? Because he was too afraid to admit that he loved her? That he needed her?

Because he *did* love her more than he loved life itself.

More than he loved his job.

Calling himself all kinds of a fool, he climbed on his horse, rode back to his cabin, and cleaned up. He had a couple of stops to make, then he was going to tell Cara how he felt.

He just hoped he wasn't too late.

CARA HAD JUST FINISHED nursing the baby when a knock sounded at the door. She tucked a strand of hair behind her ear, her heart sputtering as Mason poked his head inside.

"Can I come in?"

Hope mingled with worry as she nodded.

Tenderness softened his eyes. "How are you feeling?"

"Good," Cara said, amazed that she did feel good. But then she was probably on an adrenaline high from holding her son.

"Did you get Nacona secured?"

The glimmer of suppressed rage in his eyes didn't escape her. "We spent hours interrogating him last night but have all the proof we need. He's never getting out of prison."

Cara tried to ignore the flutter of residual fear that the memory of the night before stirred. She wanted to recall the sweet bliss of seeing her little boy for the first time, not the trauma of being held kidnapped by a murderer.

An awkwardness suddenly fell between them, making her wish she hadn't asked.

"Cara, I'm sorry I hurt you before." Mason slowly walked over to her, and she noticed the stuffed pony in his hands. "That I didn't come last night."

"Why didn't you?" Cara asked, hoping this wasn't his way of telling her that a relationship between them wouldn't work now any more than it would have nearly a year ago.

Mason made a sarcastic sound. "Because I'm a fool. I was scared."

"Scared of me?" Cara asked.

He chuckled. "Scared of disappointing you."

He leaned over and brushed his fingers across the

baby's forehead, then placed the pony in the bassinet. "This is for you, little guy. I'm your daddy."

Cara's heart swelled at the gruff sound of his voice. "Is that why you're here?" she asked softly. "You want to be a part of our little boy's life?"

He turned to her, emotions tingeing his eyes. "Yes."

She nodded, knowing she had to accept whatever he offered. She loved him too much to do anything else.

Then he moved over beside the bed and shocked her by dropping to one knee. "Mason?"

He lifted his hand and she gaped at the beautiful turquoise ring laying in the palm of his hand.

"Cara, I know I did wrong last year, but we have a baby now and I want us to do things right. Will you marry me?"

Disappointment crowded Cara's throat. "Mason, you don't have to marry me to be part of Maska's life."

His smile faded slightly. "You don't want to marry me?"

"I didn't say that," Cara said softly. "But I don't want you to propose because you feel trapped or because we have a baby together."

Mason suddenly stood, his expression oddly tender and fiercely angry at the same time. He eased down on the side of the bed and cradled her hand in his. "Listen to me, Cara. I was a fool before." He paused then gently kissed her fingers. "I love you.

I didn't propose because I feel trapped or because I think I should. I want us to be together."

Love flooded Cara's heart. "I love you, too, Mason. I've loved you for a long time."

A grin softened the hard ridges and planes of his face. "Then marry me and let's be a family."

Tears pricked at her eyes, but she refused to cry. Instead, she smiled and held out her hand, and he slipped the ring on her finger.

* * * * *

*Don't miss the next installment of
Rita Herron's gripping miniseries
BUCKING BRONC LODGE.
Look for ULTIMATE COWBOY
in February 2013
wherever Harlequin Intrigue books are sold.*

LARGER-PRINT BOOKS!
GET 2 FREE LARGER-PRINT NOVELS PLUS
2 FREE GIFTS!

◆HARLEQUIN®

INTRIGUE®

BREATHTAKING ROMANTIC SUSPENSE

The series you love are now available in

LARGER PRINT!

The books are complete and unabridged—
printed in a larger type size to make it
easier on your eyes.

HARLEQUIN
Romance

From the Heart, For the Heart

HARLEQUIN
MEDICAL™
Pulse-racing romance,
heart-racing medical drama

HARLEQUIN
INTRIGUE
BREATHTAKING ROMANTIC SUSPENSE

HARLEQUIN
Presents

Seduction and Passion Guaranteed!

HARLEQUIN
super romance

Exciting, emotional, unexpected!

Try **LARGER PRINT** today!

Visit: www.ReaderService.com
Call: 1-800-873-8635

H HARLEQUIN®

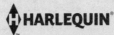 A *Romance* FOR EVERY MOOD™

www.ReaderService.com

HLPDIR13

REQUEST YOUR FREE BOOKS!

2 FREE NOVELS
PLUS 2 FREE GIFTS!

Your Partner in Crime

YES! Please send me 2 FREE novels from the Worldwide Library® series and my 2 FREE gifts (gifts are worth about $10). After receiving them, if I don't wish to receive any more books, I can return the shipping statement marked "cancel." If I don't cancel, I will receive 4 brand-new novels every month and be billed just $5.24 per book in the U.S. or $6.24 per book in Canada. That's a savings of at least 34% off the cover price. It's quite a bargain! Shipping and handling is just 50¢ per book in the U.S. and 75¢ per book in Canada.* I understand that accepting the 2 free books and gifts places me under no obligation to buy anything. I can always return a shipment and cancel at any time. Even if I never buy another book, the two free books and gifts are mine to keep forever.

414/424 WDN FVUV

Name _____ (PLEASE PRINT)

Address _____ Apt. #

City _____ State/Prov. _____ Zip/Postal Code

Signature (if under 18, a parent or guardian must sign)

Mail to the Harlequin® Reader Service:
IN U.S.A.: P.O. Box 1867, Buffalo, NY 14240-1867
IN CANADA: P.O. Box 609, Fort Erie, Ontario L2A 5X3

Want to try two free books from another line?
Call 1-800-873-8635 or visit www.ReaderService.com.

* Terms and prices subject to change without notice. Prices do not include applicable taxes. Sales tax applicable in N.Y. Canadian residents will be charged applicable taxes. Offer not valid in Quebec. This offer is limited to one order per household. Not valid for current subscribers to the Worldwide Library series. All orders subject to credit approval. Credit or debit balances in a customer's account(s) may be offset by any other outstanding balance owed by or to the customer. Please allow 4 to 6 weeks for delivery. Offer available while quantities last.

Your Privacy—The Harlequin® Reader Service is committed to protecting your privacy. Our Privacy Policy is available online at www.ReaderService.com or upon request from the Harlequin Reader Service.

We make a portion of our mailing list available to reputable third parties that offer products we believe may interest you. If you prefer that we not exchange your name with third parties, or if you wish to clarify or modify your communication preferences, please visit us at www.ReaderService.com/consumerschoice or write to us at Harlequin Reader Service Preference Service, P.O. Box 9062, Buffalo, NY 14269. Include your complete name and address.

WWLI3